WEST VIRGINIA
ROMANCES
Volume II

Tales of Young Love
in the Mountain State

By Dan Kincaid

Dan Kincaid

Copyright © 2021 by Dan B. Kincaid

ISBN	9798784280510
Published By:	Kade Holley Publishing
Editing:	Kade and Lynn Holley Shannon Lough
Cover Design:	Kade Holley Publishing and Shannon Lough
Cover Images:	From Shutterstock by Happy Stock Photo and Brocreative
Chapter Sketches:	Sarah Lough

This is a work of fiction. Names and incidents are primarily products of the author's imagination.

Printed in the United States of America.

DEDICATION

To our future great-grandchildren

REVIEWS AND READER COMMENTS

Readers will enjoy the simplistic innocence of Dan Kincaid's **West Virginia Romances: Tales of Young Love in the Mountain State**. Dan weaves tales that all will recognize regardless of their age. His stories are a nostalgic trip down memory lane for adults, and a tutorial for teens and pre-teens still finding their way through the sometimes complicated adolescent stage of life. I was particularly fond of Dan tying a budding romance into outdoor pursuits like fishing in the *Blennerhassett Romance* story. Those with ties to West Virginia will easily identify with many of the locations and references included in the stories. Young and old alike will enjoy this book.

Chris Lawrence, WV MetroNews Radio reporter/anchor and host of West Virginia Outdoors

Dan's books are a quick read with separate, individual stories of young romances. Though written with the Teenage/Young Adult audience in mind, I would recommend these books to readers of all ages and genders. Though set in West Virginia, anyone will find the stories interesting. He weaves in topics about sports, natural resources, and academics, so there is also an educational aspect to the books. I especially enjoyed reading about the West Virginia places I have visited and am familiar with that are highlighted in the stories. I also have high school classmates and a nephew who attended some of the colleges that are mentioned. I spent many summers in Morgantown and have fond memories of that city. I can relate to many of the characters in the book. After reading Volume I, I eagerly looked forward to Volume II of **West Virginia Romances: Tales of Young Love in the Mountain State** and here it is. In short, I know that you will really enjoy these stories.

Award winning author, Lorraine M. Harris

TABLE OF CONTENTS

INTRODUCTION

Stories of young love abound in the Mountain State. The stories in this book are especially suited to the young reader – both girls and boys. And even to their parents, who very possibly fell in love in West Virginia.

These four stories are primarily set in: 1) Harpers Ferry and Shepherdstown; 2) Bartow in Pocahontas County; 3) Ravenswood, Parkersburg, and Blennerhassett Island; 4) Charleston, Lewisburg, Pikeview, and Athens. Other references are made to: Boyer, Arbovale, Durbin, Point Pleasant, Charles Town, Morgantown, Spencer, Princeton, Shady Spring, Beckley, Fairmont, and perhaps a few other locations. Several colleges in the state are also mentioned.

Future volumes of this series will feature stories from all around the state.

These West Virginia romances are fictional, but very similar to situations that happen often throughout the state. And, by the way parents, these stories are G-rated.

I sincerely hope you enjoy reading these 'tales of young love in the Mountain State' and telling others about them.

- Dan Kincaid

Chapter 1

BLENNERHASSETT ROMANCE

It was the second week in July and Jay Vernon hadn't really been excited about going with his parents on this Saturday trip over to Blennerhassett Island Historical State Park. But he knew they wanted him to come along with them and his two younger sisters, Jody and Toni. It was a family outing. So, he didn't put up too much of a fuss.

However, a couple of Jay's friends in Ravenswood had wanted him to go fishing with them and, truth be told, that was what he had wanted to do. Oh well, here he was on a boat in the Ohio River.

Jay would be a senior at Ravenswood High School next school year. Jody would be entering the 9th grade in the fall, and Toni was a 6th grader. Jody had studied about Blennerhassett Island in her 8th grade

West Virginia history class and she was looking forward to this trip.

But Jay had to admit to himself that riding this sternwheeler from Parkersburg over to the island was kind of neat. He, too, had studied about Blennerhassett Island in eighth grade West Virginia history and just last year in American History, he had learned about the island and its importance in the early years of the country.

And history was definitely his favorite subject in school. In fact, he thought he would study that in college, although he wasn't sure what kind of career opportunities that field might offer. Maybe teaching, he thought. But he would have to think about that further and talk some more with the high school guidance counselors next fall as a senior before he began applying to colleges.

Jay had always wanted to attend West Virginia University in Morgantown, but he would have to find out what kind of a history program they had. And Marshall University in Huntington was always a possibility. After all, that was where his high school history teacher, Mr. Stewart, had graduated from.

As he remembered, the Blennerhassett's, Harman and Margaret, had bought part of the island and built a big mansion there soon after the Americans had defeated the British in the Revolutionary War. They were possibly more loyal to the British side, but Jay couldn't remember that for sure. They had been born in Ireland or somewhere over there and had become wealthy landowners in the colonies.

The main thing that Jay remembered was that they had met with Aaron Burr at their home, around 1805 maybe, and had discussed plans for setting up an empire and perhaps a new country in the Southwest. Burr, of course, who was then Vice-President of the United States of America, had killed Alexander Hamilton in a duel about a year earlier and he was now more or less on the run from authorities back East.

President Thomas Jefferson learned of the Blennerhassett–Burr plan to possibly invade the Southwest and to set up a new country somewhere around the present state of Texas. He ordered them arrested for treason. Jay couldn't remember all of the details, but Burr was eventually acquitted. However, he and Blennerhassett were pretty much ruined from that point on. Burr fled to England, but eventually returned to America where he lived in poverty with various medical ailments until his death several years later.

The Blennerhassett's fled their island mansion, which was subsequently occupied and plundered by the Virginia militia. It was mysteriously burned to the ground a few years later. Harman Blennerhassett lost his fortune and eventually died penniless back in England. Margaret went there, too, but she eventually returned to America after her husband died. She also lived in poverty in New York and passed away several years later.

Jay was sometimes amazed by how much history he remembered. But, after all, it was his favorite subject. His parents didn't lean that way at all. His dad, Greg, worked for the State of West Virginia, helping manage the Cedar Lakes Conference Center near Ripley. His mother, Gina, was a nurse, who was excellent in the medical and science fields. But if there was anything she hated worse than studying geography, it was history. Despite all of this, Jay loved history and wanted to study it further in college. His parents told him they weren't sure what he would do with a degree in history, but they couldn't change his mind.

But now, the 20-minute boat ride to Blennerhassett Island was nearly over and they were docking. They would hopefully get a quick bite to eat at the concession building before walking up to visit the restored mansion, which was run by the West Virginia Division of State Parks.

Jay was actually looking forward to visiting the mansion and looking around, learning more about the history of the island. Tours of the mansion were set up very well with people dressed in period costumes and explaining things in several rooms of the mansion. As they toured the mansion, one young lady was assigned to lead the group that Jay was in. She seemed to be about his age and he wasn't sure if he was imagining it or not, but she seemed to glance at him from time to time and smile. Of course, he smiled back. She was a very cute girl after all.

At the end of the mansion tour, Jay eased over and asked the girl if she was a high school student and where she was from.

"Yes, I'll be a senior in high school this fall and I go to school across the river in Belpre," she said. "Are you from Parkersburg?"

"No, we live in Ravenswood and I go to high school down there," Jay replied. "I'll be a senior, too. How did you get a job like this?"

"My uncle operates the sternwheeler and he had some pull to help me get this summer job," she answered. "And I just love it. I lead groups on tours here, usually four or five days a week. It's a lot better than working in a fast-food restaurant."

"That's for sure," Jay agreed. "By the way what's your name?"

"Misty Conley," she said. "What's yours?"

"I'm Jay Vernon, at your service, Miss Conley," he replied, as they both laughed.

"Well, Mr. Vernon, how have you enjoyed your visit so far?" Misty asked, grinning.

"It's been great," said Jay. "I actually love history and I plan to study it in college. And also, it's been even better now that I've met the lovely Misty Conley."

Again, they both laughed.

"Well, I have to get back to work," Misty said. "There's another group coming in that I have to lead through the mansion. If you have time, Mr. Vernon, be sure to swing by here and say goodbye before you head back," she said, winking at Jay.

"I definitely will," Jay said enthusiastically.

She winked at me, Jay thought. I think. No, it was definitely a wink. She winked at me. This is better than going fishing with the guys, for sure.

"What were you and that young lady talking about," Gina asked Jay, when he walked back over to where his parents were standing.

"Fishing, mom. She likes to go fishing," Jay said with a smile on his face.

"Oh, I'm sure," said Gina. "Seriously, it seemed like you had a long conversation."

"Well, believe it or not, it wasn't a long conversation, but we were talking about history and

Blennerhassett Island," said Jay. "She lives over in Belpre, Ohio and her uncle operates the sternwheel boat that we just rode on. She'll be a senior next school year and her uncle helped her get this summer job. She leads visitor groups around the mansion several days a week."

"My, but that seems like a lot of information to have gathered with just a short conversation," Gina replied, with a grin. "And I guess you don't even know her name, right?"

"Now that you asked," Jay said sheepishly, "her name is Misty Conley. And that's all I want to say about this."

His sister, Jody, who had been standing beside their mother, said playfully, "When are you getting married?"

Jay gently pushed Jody and said, "Gee, what fun to have two younger sisters. Is it now that I tell you to mind your own business?"

"Okay, kids, that's enough," their mother said. "Let's see what else this island has to offer. Your dad and Toni are over in the gift shop. I think he wanted to walk around and look things over. There are trails to walk and a wagon ride available. There's also another restored home here that was built around 1802 and was moved over from Belpre. I'd like to see that myself. And since your dad works at Cedar Lakes, he's always interested in what other state parks and recreation areas look like."

After a short hike, a horse-drawn wagon ride, and visiting the restored Putnam-Houser House, the Vernon's were all tired and ready to board the sternwheeler and head back over to where their car was parked in Parkersburg.

"Wait, just a second," said Jay. "I need to go check on something really quick up at the mansion. It's about history."

"I'm sure," said Jody. "But I wouldn't call it history."

As Jay got back up to the mansion, Misty stepped away from her last group for a minute. "I was afraid I had missed you," she said.

"No, I hadn't forgotten," Jay replied, "but we're getting ready to leave. Let's exchange phone numbers, if you're all right with that."

"That would be great," she said. "And what all did you see and do on the island today?"

"Well, the mansion tour was very interesting," said Jay. "We bought a few souvenirs, took a short hike and wagon ride, and we visited the restored house, too. Being a history buff, I liked all of it. But the best thing for me today was meeting our lovely tour guide, Misty Conley."

Misty blushed and said, "I was hoping that was the case. You were my favorite visitor of the day, too. Or the whole week, for that matter. Will you call me soon?"

"You can count on it. Gotta run now to catch that sternwheeler or your uncle may leave without us," he laughed. "Oh, I almost forgot, here's my phone number. I wrote it on this brochure. Let me have yours."

After getting Misty's phone number, Jay ran back down to the boat landing, where his parents were waiting to board. "Did you find out about the history thing you wanted to check on?" Gina asked.

"Uh, yes," said Jay.

"Did you get her phone number?" Jody kiddingly asked.

"What are they talking about?" Toni asked her dad.

"Beats me," said Greg. "They keep me in the dark about some things."

Jay and his mother made eye contact and he slowly nodded his head, yes, as she smiled.

*　　*　　*　　*　　*　　*　　*

Everyone was pretty quiet on the drive back to Ravenswood. They were tired after a long, but enjoyable day.

Not long after they got back home, Jay's two friends, Dean and Charlie, stopped by to tell him about their fishing trip. They had driven over to the McClintic Ponds near Point Pleasant for the day. Between them, they had caught three catfish, two largemouth bass, and many nice sized sunfish. Charlie had even caught one small muskie. They seemed to have had a great day. The McClintic Wildlife Area, which included over 20 ponds to fish in, was only a 45-minute drive from Ravenswood and it was a favorite fishing destination for area anglers.

"We'll go over there again, when we can all find the time," said Dean. "I'll bet you wish you could have come with us instead of going to Blennerhassett Island."

"Well, I hated to miss the fishing trip, for sure," said Jay. "But the Blennerhassett trip was fun, too. You both know I like history and there's a lot of that over there. I had a good time."

"What's so great about visiting an island in the middle of the Ohio River?" asked Charlie. "Unless it's part of a fishing trip."

"Well, you'll never know," Jay said, thinking back to meeting Misty. "You'll never know."

Dean and Charlie just looked at each other and shook their heads. "See you later," they said as they left. Getting into their car, Charlie said to Dean, "Sometimes that Jay doesn't make a lick of sense. Last night when we talked, he was all upset about having to go to Blennerhassett Island instead of going fishing with us. And now he acts like it was the greatest thing ever. I don't know what's wrong with him."

*   *   *   *   *   *   *

Jay waited until Tuesday to call Misty. She had told him that her workdays varied some, but that she was usually off on Tuesdays and Wednesdays. Jay worked through the week down at the Ravenswood City Park, normally from 10:00 a.m. to 3:00 p.m., helping run recreation programs for the area youths.

He waited until 9:30 to call Misty and he could tell that she was still not quite wide awake. But she was happy to hear from him. He explained that he had to go to work, but would call her that evening if that was all right. She said that was great and that if he would call her around 8:30 p.m., they could talk for quite a while.

Jay went on down to the park, but all he could think about was talking with Misty later that day. He didn't even really know her yet, but she had sure captured his attention and his thoughts.

The kids that Jay worked with at the park were mostly younger than 12 years old and he enjoyed it. Today, they split into two groups and had a tug of war. Then, he divided them up into teams for relay races, which they always loved. And the final activity for the day was a scavenger hunt. That had been suggested and organized by the Recreation Director, who was Jay's boss. In between all of the activities, there was adequate rest time, a break with snacks and drinks, and some free time, too, for the kids to climb on the playground equipment.

Jay went home at 3;00 p.m., took a shower, and laid down for a nap before their evening family meal, which was usually around 6:00. After dinner, he told his parents that he was going up to his room and read for a while; and then make some phone calls to his friends.

Practically right at the exact time that the second hand on Jay's wall clock indicated it was 8:30 p.m., Jay eagerly dialed Misty's phone number. Misty answered on the second ring.

"Hello, Jay," she said, recognizing his name that she had programmed into her cell phone. "My, but you are certainly punctual. When you say that you'll call at 8:30, you really mean it."

"I've been thinking about it all day," said Jay. "In fact, this is the highlight of my day."

"How do you know that?" Misty asked. "We haven't even talked yet."

"No, but let's get started," he said. "How was your day?"

"It was good. I slept in until 9:30 this morning, which is when you first called me. Then, I helped with some things around the house, talked with a couple of my girlfriends, took some books back to the Belpre Library, and spent the rest of the day thinking about your call," Misty said. "How about you?"

Jay told Misty about his day working at the City Park, taking a nap, having a family meal, and then waiting until it was time to call her – at exactly 8:30 p.m. He also told her about the fishing trip he had missed going on with his friends, Dean and Charlie, on the day that he had met her on Blennerhassett Island.

"I'm sorry you had to come to Blennerhassett Island and miss going fishing with your friends," Misty said.

"Don't be sorry," Jay said. "I love to fish, but I can do that anytime. It worked out well since I had the chance to meet a pretty girl from Belpre who was a tour guide on the island."

Misty giggled and replied, "Well, I'm sure glad you came to Blennerhassett. What all does your job entail at the Ravenswood Park?"

"It's just a small park along the Ohio River and it's run by the City of Ravenswood," explained Jay. "I mainly help out with summer programs for the younger kids. We do races, have water balloon fights, and all kinds of activities for them. And we always have a snack time, too. Sometimes when there aren't activities scheduled, I help out the city crew with weed trimming or painting or minor maintenance around the park. There are picnic tables, playground equipment, parking areas, and a boat ramp. It takes quite a bit of effort to keep it all looking nice."

"Sounds like an interesting summer job," said Misty. "And I meant to ask, where do you and your friends go fishing and what do you catch?"

"Well, of course, there is the Ohio River, where we fish sometimes. There is also a stream that empties into the Ohio River near the park, and a couple of other streams not far away where we fish, too. We usually catch bluegills, catfish, and a few bass," he explained. "My friends went over to the McClintic Ponds near Point Pleasant the other day when I was at Blennerhassett Island. They said they caught bass, catfish, bluegills, and a muskie. There are several ponds over there and it's a favorite place for people around here to go fishing.

"One of the best places to fish near here," continued Jay, "is over at the Racine Lock and Dam on the Ohio side. It's only a half hour or less from Ravenswood and me and my dad go over there from time to time. You can catch about anything at Racine – sauger, striped bass, catfish, smallmouth bass, hybrid stripers, white bass, you name it. Sorry to get so wound up talking about fishing, but next to history, it's my favorite thing. Have you ever been fishing?" he asked.

"Have I ever been fishing? You wouldn't believe it, but my dad and I used to go fishing all of the time, especially when I was younger," said Misty. "We don't go as often anymore because I've been working and involved with a lot of school activities."

"But dad fishes in bass tournaments and he has fished at all of the nearby lock and dams – Belleville, Racine, Willow Island, and others, too. So, yes, I have been fishing and I love it. I even caught a 5-pound largemouth bass a few years ago. Dad couldn't believe it when I landed that monster. He got it mounted and it's in his den. I didn't really want it in my room......and neither did mom," laughed Misty.

"Wow," said Jay. "That's a bigger bass than I've ever caught. I knew there was something special about you."

Jay and Misty talked for over an hour about their upcoming senior year in high school, plans for college, their friends, their jobs, things they liked to do, and, yes, more about fishing. Jay couldn't believe Misty liked fishing so much. Most of the girls he knew were not interested in that at all. Before they hung up, they decided that they would meet at the mall in Parkersburg the first chance they got.

Misty said that since she had worked a couple of days extra over the past few weeks, her boss promised that she could have a weekend day off soon. Misty planned to ask if she could have Sunday off and told Jay that she would let him know in a day or two. They agreed to talk Thursday evening, again at exactly 8:30 p.m.

On Thursday when they talked, Misty told Jay that she was able to get Sunday off. They planned to meet at the mall in Parkersburg on Sunday at 1:30 p.m.

Jay was excited and that was all he could think about for the rest of the week. His mother, Gina, noticed that he was kind of pre-occupied with his thoughts, but had been in a good mood lately.

"My, but you've sure been in a good mood the past few days," she said to Jay. "What's up? Has it anything to do with the 'mysterious' phone calls you've made recently?"

"Maybe," Jay said. "But, mom, you know I'm usually in a good mood anyway."

"That's true," his mother said. "But this just seems different. Seriously, what's up? Another fishing trip planned? Or thoughts of Blennerhassett Island? I know how much you like history.......and mansion tours, among other things," she smiled.

"You know me better than anyone does," Jay grinned. "I guess you've figured out that I've been talking with Misty Conley on the phone. We have a lot in common. And she's so easy to talk with. We're going to meet at the Parkersburg mall Sunday afternoon and get to know each other better. And I can't wait!"

"At least that explains your good mood lately," Gina said.

*   *   *   *   *   *   *

The Vernon's attended early church service on Sunday morning and on the way home, Jay's dad said, "Hey, Jay, want to head over to the Racine Dam and do a little fishing this afternoon? I hear the sauger and white bass have been hitting like crazy."

"Oh, gee dad, I'd love to, but I promised to meet a friend this afternoon," Jay said.

"Well, see if he wants to come along, too. That would be fine," said Greg.

"It's not really like that, dad. I have to meet this friend in Parkersburg at the mall. He, or I mean she, will be there at 1:30. We've had it planned for a few days," explained Jay.

Greg turned to his wife and said that there were sure a lot of things going on lately that he didn't understand. Gina smiled and assured Greg that she was aware of the mall meeting and that everything would be all right. She would tell him more about it after they got home.

Jay took a quick shower to freshen up a little bit, changed into more comfortable clothes, and before long he was ready to head for the mall. It would only take about 45 minutes to get there, but he left shortly after noon. He wanted to already be there whenever Misty arrived. They had planned to meet in the food court and get something to eat, too.

Jay arrived just after 1:00 p.m. and staked out a good seat where he could watch for Misty coming in the door. And about 1:20 there she was. Wow, she was pretty, even more so than he remembered when they first met on Blennerhassett Island. He waved her on over and then gave her a short hug, which she didn't seem to mind at all.

"Boy, it's sure good to see you, Misty," Jay said excitedly. "I thought today would never get here. You look great, by the way."

"Well thank you, Mr. Vernon," Misty said, and they both laughed. "Or should I just call you Jay?"

"You know that Jay is fine," he grinned. "Let's get something to eat while we talk. Then we can walk around the mall, if that's okay with you."

"Sounds good," said Misty.

They split a large sub sandwich and one of those over-sized chocolate chip cookies, while they both had iced tea. As they talked it seemed to Jay like they had known each other for a long time because the conversation came easy. Misty was fun to talk with and she was very interesting.

Jay learned that Misty was a good student, which didn't surprise him, and that she was a member of the National Honor Society. Jay was, too, so it was good that they both took their studies seriously.

"What do you plan to do after graduation?" Jay asked. "I guess you'll go to college."

"Well, I've enjoyed my work at Blennerhassett Island so much," Misty explained, "that I've just about decided to study parks and recreation in college and try to eventually work for a state or national park as an interpretive specialist or park ranger. What about you?"

"I hope to major in history," Jay said. "I love everything about history. My folks don't think the job market is great for history majors, but I'm not sure that's true. I plan to talk with my history teacher, Mr. Stewart, some more about that."

"Where would you go to college to study your subject?" asked Jay.

"I think I will go to Marshall, down in Huntington," Misty answered. "They have a good program in that field, leading to a Bachelor of Science degree in Natural Resources and Recreation Management."

"I have an aunt who lives just outside of Huntington and she works in the admissions department at Marshall," Misty continued. "She's not sure yet about how I could get in-state tuition, but she thinks there may be a way. She's working on that. She told me that WVU already has in place a reciprocal agreement with Ohio for tuition and there have been talks with Marshall to start that, also.

"Plus, I can stay with her for at least the first year or two, which will help on finances," she explained. "I might also be able to qualify as an in-state student by doing that. My grades are such that my guidance counselor thinks I will qualify for a few scholarships, too. So, I'm pretty sure I'll go to Marshall."

"Well, that settles it then," Jay said. "I'm going to Marshall, too. I had been wavering back and forth between West Virginia University and Marshall, but hello Huntington, here I come! After all, my history teacher Mr. Stewart went to Marshall, so I'll talk with him some more about majoring in history there."

"That would be great," said Misty, "but let's get to know each other better before we start making any major plans."

"I agree," said Jay, "but for starters I think this is a good early plan, don't you?"

"Yes, I do," Misty replied. "Now, let's walk around the mall some."

The couple walked and talked for the next hour and a half, holding hands for the last 30 minutes. Jay couldn't believe how much Misty knew about fishing, as well as quite a bit about area history, too. And he had to admit that being a park ranger or naturalist or anything along those lines was interesting to him, also. He sure was glad that his parents had made him go with them on the Blennerhassett Island trip earlier.

"I guess we'd better head back to our homes," said Misty. "It's almost four o'clock."

"I guess so," said Jay. "The time sure went fast, didn't it? Oh, by the way, sometime I want to see that 5-pound bass you caught."

"Not a problem," Misty said. "After all, dad has it mounted and hanging on the wall in his den. Maybe we could go fishing with him sometime, too."

"That would be great," Jay said. "And maybe my dad and I could meet you all down at the Racine Dam to go fishing someday. I sure hope so."

"Me, too," Misty replied. "That would be fun."

They were almost back to the food court and it was time to say goodbye. Jay gave Misty a gentle hug and decided to kiss her on the cheek. She didn't appear to mind and kept her face close to his, so he decided to give her a quick kiss on the lips. They pulled apart slowly, both with smiles on their faces.

"I had a great time," said Misty.

"So did I," Jay said. "I'll call you Tuesday or Wednesday. Goodbye, and drive carefully."

"You, too," said Misty.

Jay was on cloud nine all the way home. When he entered the house, his mother asked him how the afternoon went. Fine, he told her, and that he would fill her in more about it later. Right now, he said he had to go look up some things about Marshall University on his computer and also give his history teacher, Mr. Stewart, a call.

"Okay," his mom said, looking at him quizzically. This should be an interesting talk later, she thought.

By the time he got in touch with his history teacher and then researched some things about Marshall University, it was too late to talk with his mother about how the day had gone. He would do that tomorrow after he talked with Mr. Stewart, who had agreed to meet with him at Ravenswood High School in the morning at 8:00 a.m. to talk about college. He would have plenty of time to get to work at the park by 10:00. Jay was really happy about how things were going.

* * * * * * *

Jay met Mr. Stewart bright and early Monday morning at the high school and they went into the teacher's lounge to talk.

"So, what's up, Jay?" Mr. Stewart asked. "Last night you said something about wanting to know more about careers for college history majors. I knew you liked history, but we haven't discussed a career yet. I can tell you what I know, but then you'll want to talk with the guidance counselors, too."

"I talked with them a little bit last spring about maybe majoring in history in college," Jay told him. "But they're kind of like my parents are with 'there aren't many jobs in that field.' Everyone seems to point good students toward, what is it, STEM? – science, technology, engineering, and math. I know those are important fields, and I'm good in those subjects, too, but my first love is studying history."

"Well, I know what you mean," said Mr. Stewart. "Even back when I was going to college, my parents and everyone else said 'what are you going to do with a history degree,' teach? So, yes, that's what I ended up doing; but I like teaching high school students and I like history, so it's a good fit for me. Also, I get to coach baseball, which is something I enjoy, too."

"I think I would enjoy teaching at the high school level, too," said Jay, "but I've been told that it is sometimes hard to find an opening in that field. What other options would I have with a degree in history and is Marshall a good school for history majors?"

"Yes, Marshall has a very good history department," Mr. Stewart explained. "I know several of the professors there and they are top notch. I even went to school with one of them in my undergraduate days. You can concentrate on various specialties, like early American history, European history of certain eras, other types of world history, World War II history, or just about anything you want to specialize in. They will work with you to develop a slate of courses and independent study to focus on your interests. Marshall also has developed an excellent reputation for

Appalachian history, for students interested in that area of study," he explained.

"And yes," he continued, "it can sometimes be difficult to get into a high school history teaching slot; but a good college history graduate with good recommendations, if they're patient, can usually line up a teaching position."

"That all sounds promising," Jay said. "What other options are there for history majors?"

"The first thing would be that if you're a top student, which in all honesty I was not, you could continue in college to work on a master's degree and PhD in a specific area of study," said Mr. Stewart. "That could set you up for a college teaching position or a research position or a combination of both. Some friends of mine actually do quite a bit of research and publish books or write for magazines, but they also combine that with being a university professor. The colleges like to have professors on their staffs that publish a lot of their findings. And sometimes all they have to do beyond their research and writing is to teach one course each semester. Or two at the most. They even get to take a sabbatical from teaching from time to time to continue their outside work and research, but still remain on the university payroll."

"That would be great," said Jay. "What else could a history major do?"

"Really, there are unlimited opportunities," Mr. Stewart told him. "There are more than a few lawyers who had undergraduate degrees in history. I even know one lady who got her history degree, then took an extra year of science and math courses and got accepted into medical school. She's now in family practice in Columbus, Ohio. And another one of her friends up there who had a history degree ended up becoming a veterinarian. That person now works primarily with horses down in the Lexington, Kentucky area and even does some history work with various horse racing museums and non-profit organizations on the side. It can all be done, if you have the interest."

"How in the world did a history major end up working as a horse veterinarian?" Jay asked.

"Well, what I was told is that she was working on a master's degree in history at Ohio State University and it concerned the history of horses in this country, how they got here, what parts of the world they came from, the origins of different breeds, and so on," explained Mr. Stewart. "She had always loved horses and done some trail riding with her family. That's what spurred the idea for her research, which was approved by her faculty advisors. The further she got into her research the more she thought about how she would love to get a job working with horses fulltime.

"Ohio State has a Veterinarian Program, so she went over and talked with them about her interest. One thing led to another, and by taking a few extra courses, she was accepted into Vet School. So, there you go, a veterinarian with a bachelor's degree in history.

"Let's see, what else?" Mr. Stewart continued. "Some history majors have gone into public relations or public affairs jobs. Others have become park rangers, librarians, or even high school English/Literature teachers with just a little extra course work. Many have gone into business in various fields, including sales and marketing positions; or even, heaven forbid, politics, either running for office or becoming a political strategist or advisor. I also know a sports editor who was a history major in college. He played college baseball at Marietta College in Ohio and afterward began working as a sportswriter for the newspaper in Parkersburg, which is how I got to know him. He eventually worked his way up to become sports editor for a mid-sized newspaper in northeastern Ohio that does not only print journalism, but a substantial amount of on-line and electronic sports journalism."

"So, there you have it. You could do just about anything with a history degree if you study hard and put forth great effort. Does this help you with your questions?" Mr. Stewart said.

"Oh, definitely," Jay said excitedly. "It has opened up my mind to more possibilities than I ever imagined. I think it has helped convince me more than ever that I want to study history in college."

"Well, I'm glad to have helped. And I certainly enjoyed talking with you about it. But don't forget to talk with the guidance counselors, too. I don't want them to think I'm trying to steal some of their work. They can also help you with scholarships, applications, and anything along those lines," Mr. Stewart said. "But I'd be glad to offer you a reference or recommendation if that would be helpful to you."

"Gee, thanks," said Jay. "I really appreciate that."

"I meant to ask you," Mr. Stewart went on, "what made you decide to focus on Marshall? I seem to remember that you and your folks were big WVU fans."

"Well, I have a friend who plans to attend Marshall," Jay explained. "And I just thought it would be good if I could go there, too."

"Oh, I see," said Mr. Stewart. "Is it someone I know from this high school?"

"No," replied Jay. "She, or I mean, 'they' attend school up in Belpre, Ohio."

"I understand," Mr. Stewart smiled. "Well, even if things don't work out with her, or I mean 'them,' you can rest assured that you will get an excellent education at Marshall University."

Jay felt very good about his talk with Mr. Stewart. It sure gave him some things to think about and some information that he could use to help convince his parents, and even the guidance counselors, that majoring in history would be a good idea. He could also share this new information with Misty; yes, the lovely Miss Misty Conley, who seemed to occupy a lot of his thoughts lately. It was now 9:30 a.m. and Jay needed to go on over to the park for his ten o'clock job.

Later that evening after dinner, Jay's mother asked him about his Sunday visit with Misty and what was up with him and Mr. Stewart.

"I just wanted to talk with him about his career as a history teacher, how he liked it, and his being a history major at Marshall," Jay explained. "He told me that Marshall has a strong history department and it would be a good school to attend for that major."

"That's interesting," Gina observed. "Why Marshall all of a sudden? I thought you were wanting to attend WVU."

"No reason," Jay responded. "I just want to explore all options. And Marshall is a good school. You and dad wouldn't mind me going there, would you?"

"No, I guess not," she said. "It would be closer to us, maybe only half as far away as Morgantown. But we're still not sold on you majoring in history. Jobs in that field are scarce and I don't think they pay much either."

Jay proceeded to tell his mother more about his meeting with Mr. Stewart and all of the job possibilities for history majors. She seemed impressed that Jay had looked into things that thoroughly.

"And as far as pay goes, you and dad have always said the most important thing with a job is that you like it and you're happy," said Jay. "I even remember dad being offered higher paying jobs a couple of times, but he decided against them because he loves working at Cedar Lakes."

"I guess that's true," said Gina. "Let's talk with your dad about all of this and your recent change of mind about going to Marshall instead of WVU. And let me ask, does this have anything to do with Misty Conley? This all seems to have occurred since you've been talking with her. Is she going to go to Marshall?"

"Well, she doesn't have anything to do with me wanting to major in history, but, yes, she does plan to attend Marshall," admitted Jay.

"I see," Gina smiled. "Well, that's all right, I guess, but don't let that influence where you want to go to school. You only recently met her and who knows if you'll even be together in another year or two. Sometimes these things don't last and you'll need to be happy with your choice of a college."

"I know, mom," Jay said. "You're right, but Misty and I seem to be meant for each other. We have so much in common. And, man, is she a lovely girl; beautiful, I'd say. She said that she thinks I'm cute, too. I guess we'll learn more about each other during this coming year. And if we go fishing a few times."

Jay's mother just shook her head about the fishing comment and told Jay they would talk about this more with his dad later.

Gina talked with her husband, Greg, and decided that they would leave the decision to Jay. After all, it was his life and they would support him in his choice of a major and a college. Greg had graduated from WVU with a degree in accounting before he went to work for the state. He was now the head of the business management and personnel section at Cedar Lakes. He had always hoped that his kids would attend WVU, too, but Marshall was fine. Maybe Jody or Toni would end up going to WVU.

Gina had obtained her Registered Nursing degree from the WVU branch at Parkersburg and she was fine with Jay attending either WVU at Morgantown or Marshall in Huntington. She was still a little concerned about Jay wanting to study history in college, however, but both Greg and Jay had convinced her to let that concern go. History it would be, she thought. She just hoped that his reason for wanting to go to Marshall, in the form of the 'lovely' fisherwoman Misty

Conley, would not end up breaking his heart. Gina would certainly hope for the best on that.

Over the next few days, Jay had a chance to tell his dad about Misty and her father going fishing together for many years, and about the five-pound largemouth bass she had caught. Misty had also told Jay that her dad said he would take them fishing in his bass boat in the Ohio River, if they would like that.

"I've caught a few largemouths bigger than five pounds, but not many," Greg said. "But that's sure a nice one. She must good be at fishing."

"I think she is," said Jay. "How about you, me, and Misty going down to Racine soon and fishing below the dam?"

"Sure," said Greg. "You two pick a day and we'll go; I can even take a day off work if necessary."

"Also," Jay said, "her dad wants to take Misty and me fishing in his bass boat in the Belleville pool of the Ohio River. Are you okay with that?"

"That's fine. If he fishes in bass tournaments, I'm sure he knows what he's doing. Just wear life vests and be careful," his dad said.

*   *   *   *   *   *   *

Over the next few weeks before school started, Jay and Misty talked several times a week. They also met at the mall two more times, once going to a movie while they were there. Misty visited the Vernon's in Ravenswood once and Jay visited the Conley's in Belpre once, too. Everyone seemed to get along very well. And yes, he had a chance to see her five-pound bass. What an impressive fish!

Jay and his dad took Misty fishing at the Racine Dam once and to everyone's surprise, except Misty's, she caught more fish than the other two combined. Jay and his dad each caught a couple of saugers and Greg also caught two white bass. Misty caught seven fish – four white bass, two saugers, and the biggest one of the day, a 24-inch striped bass.

"My, oh my, Misty, you sure are a good fisherman, or I mean fisherwoman," said Greg. "Jay told me you were good and now I believe it. Great job!"

"Thank you, Mr. Vernon," she said. "I love to fish. Dad and I have been doing it since I was young. And it's okay to call me a fisherman, instead of a fisherwoman. Fisherman seems to sound better to me."

"Told you, dad," said Jay. "Isn't she great?"

Greg looked at Misty and they both smiled at Jay's remark. It was obvious that he was 'hooked' on Misty.

On the day that Jay and Misty went fishing with her dad, Fred Conley, their luck was not quite so good.

Misty hooked one small channel catfish and Jay caught two bass - one a largemouth and one a smallmouth along the shore. Mr. Conley didn't fish much, concentrating on steering the boat for the other two to fish. But they sure had a great time.

"Misty tells me that you like to fish and that you like to study history," said Fred.

"Yes," said Jay. "And my plans are to attend Marshall next year and major in history."

"Well, Misty plans to go there, too, so maybe you two will see each other down there," Fred said, grinning at his daughter.

"Maybe so," replied Misty, smiling at Jay.

*   *   *   *   *   *   *

Once school started Misty and Jay weren't able to see each other very often during the week, but they still talked on the phone as often as possible. And Misty attended two of Ravenswood's football games with Jay – an away game at Williamstown and a home game against their big rival, Ripley.

Jay went with Misty to two of Belpre's football games, also – an away game against Meigs in Pomeroy, Ohio and a home game versus Federal Hocking.

Students at both schools began to see them together and hear about this budding romance between

Jay and Misty. They attended each other's Homecoming Dance, went to some basketball games together during the winter months, and planned to go to each school's prom. The excitement of high school graduation came and went and soon thoughts turned to attending college.

Jay had received his acceptance letter from Marshall in mid-January and Misty got hers in early February. Her aunt had been able to list her residence as Misty's, with full knowledge of the Admissions Director, and that was a welcome relief. Misty would have to move to Huntington a couple of weeks before school began, get her West Virginia driver's license, and fill out a few forms with her aunt.

Jay and Misty both received scholarships that ended up paying the bulk of their fees for the first year of college, with the expectation of continuing those scholarships as long as they kept up their grades. It paid to be an excellent student with a high grade point average, belong to the National Honor Society, and have good scores on the college entrance tests.

Once classes began at Marshall, Jay met with his advisor from the history department and Misty met with hers from natural resources & recreation. Both programs were excited to gain two such excellent students. The advisors were also able to talk with each of them about summer jobs and internships that would be available as they progressed in their studies.

Jay and Misty spent as much time with each other on campus as possible and even studied together sometimes. Jay was able to bring a car to school, but Misty wouldn't have one for another year. She rode to and from school each day with her aunt. Occasionally, Jay was able to take her back to her aunt's house in the evening. He became somewhat of a regular visitor there and enjoyed some good home-cooked meals. And they all got along great.

Jay and Misty became closer and closer; they even began talking more about their future after college. About once a month they returned for the weekend to Ravenswood and Belpre to visit with their families; after which it was back to Huntington to continue their studies. Everyone began to think that this was a match made in heaven; one of those pairings that was just meant to be.

And it had all begun when Jay missed a fishing trip with his buddies, went to Blennerhassett Island with his family, and then first met the 'lovely' Miss Misty Conley.

Chapter 2

POCAHONTAS COUNTY CONNECTION

Just when she thought things couldn't get any worse, Valerie Taylor's dad, Vince, had told the family an hour earlier that they would be moving to Bartow, West Virginia. He had been promoted to be the District Ranger for the Greenbrier District of the Monongahela National Forest. She had just broken up with her boyfriend, Tony, yesterday and now this.

The move itself had not come as a complete surprise. Just a month ago, her dad had been told by his supervisor that he was being considered for one of three District Ranger positions in the U.S Forest Service's Eastern Region. Those positions were located in Athens, Ohio on the Wayne National Forest; Cadillac, Michigan on the Huron-Manistee National Forest; and Bartow, West Virginia on the Monongahela National Forest. For his career advancement this was a move that Vince had anticipated was coming.

Vince had expressed his preference for the Athens location, but he knew that was a long shot. He was currently the Assistant Ranger on the Wayne National Forest's Ironton District and it was normal policy to promote Rangers to another forest. It was not always true, but, more often than not, the main office handled promotions that way. Vince knew that moving from Ironton to Athens would be easier on the family than a move to either of the other two locations, but he would do whatever the Forest Service wanted. He was definitely loyal to the agency.

After Vince told the family about the three possible locations, Valerie had researched all of them. If they had to move, she thought that Athens would be the best place of the three possibilities.

Athens would be in the same state and was only a couple of hours from Ironton. Also, Ohio University (OU) was located in Athens and there would be plenty of things to do there. Since Valerie was going to enter her junior year in high school, she was beginning to think about colleges and OU would be a definite possibility. Athens was a little bigger than Ironton, but with Ashland, Kentucky just across the Ohio River from Ironton and Huntington, West Virginia just a half hour away, there had always been plenty of places to shop and things for teenagers to do. Still, if the family had to move, Valerie thought Athens would work for her.

She had read about Cadillac, too. It seemed like a nice place and was about the same size as Ironton. The main drawback for this Michigan location was the climate – long winters with lots of snow and cold weather. When Valerie was younger, before her dad took the job in Ironton, they had lived in Medford, Wisconsin where he worked on the Chequamegon National Forest. When they moved to Ironton, the whole family agreed that they would prefer not to live that far north again.

Still, Valerie thought that a move to Cadillac would be better than a move to Bartow, West Virginia. She had researched that town and noted that the population was listed as 99. If the Taylor family of five moved there, it would raise the population to 104! Whoopee! It was also cold in the winter and snowed quite a bit, too, she learned from her research. Definitely not a place for a high school girl to live. No, let's mark that one off the list, Valerie thought to herself at the time, and keep my fingers crossed for Athens or Cadillac.

But now this. Vince had gathered the family to announce that he would be taking the District Ranger position in Bartow. It was now early June, and his reporting date for the new job was August 3.

They wouldn't have to find a house in Bartow because there was a Forest Service home for the Ranger to live in. That solved one problem. But Vince promised the family that they would take at least one weekend trip to Bartow to check things out before the actual move. He figured it was about a five-hour drive. Since school was out, they could make it a three- or four-day weekend and explore a little while they were over there.

Vince and his wife Rita thought that their two sons, Brian and Phil, ages 9 and 11, would adjust and might actually enjoy living in an area with lots of forests, and plenty of hiking and fishing. But for 16-year-old Valerie, they knew things would be difficult. She was very involved in activities at Ironton High School, made good grades, played volleyball, and ran track. After Vince had told the family about the upcoming move to Bartow, Valerie had started crying, ran to her room, and locked the door.

About an hour later, Rita had finally convinced Valerie to open the door so they could talk. "Mom, I'm not going to go," Valerie said. "It's in the middle of nowhere and I won't have any friends or anything to do. And I saw on the map that the high school was like 20 or 30 miles from Bartow. I'm just not going to go. I'll stay here with Janelle or Patti's family. I know they would let me do that," Valerie said through her tears.

"I know this isn't the location you wanted," Rita said, "but we have to go as a family, and it's what is best for your dad's career."

"Please, mom, please don't make me go," Valerie pleaded.

"Look honey, we have to keep an open mind," explained her mother. "If we try to make the best of it, maybe we'll find that it's our favorite place ever."

"I doubt that," Valerie replied, sobbing. "They probably don't even have a track team or a volleyball team. I'm so upset!"

"Well, at least you won't have to break up with a boyfriend," said Rita, regretting almost instantly that she had even said that.

"Oh, mom, why would you say such a thing," breaking into a full out cry.

*   *   *   *   *   *   *

It was now the July 4th weekend and the Taylor's were taking their first visit to Bartow. Since they would be moving into a government-owned house, Vince was not approved for an official house-hunting trip. The Forest Supervisor, however, had given him permission to stay in the house for the holiday weekend so that the family could look around, meet some of their fellow employees, and begin getting used to their new surroundings.

Vince had taken a day of annual leave on Friday, so that they could drive over to Bartow before the office closed and pick up the keys to the house. The Taylor's arrived just after lunch and Vince picked up the house keys from Stan Jamison, the District Clerk for the Greenbrier Ranger District.

"Glad to meet you, and welcome to Bartow," Jamison said to Vince. "Our previous Ranger has been gone since last March, so we're in need of having a boss around here."

"Well, thanks Stan," Vince said. "I don't think of myself as a boss, though; I think we can all work together as a team."

"That'll be just fine," Stan replied. "I think that's the way we all prefer it, too."

"Most of the employees took a vacation day today," continued Jamison, "so that they could have a four-day weekend, with Monday being the official holiday. You'll get to meet them and their families Sunday afternoon up at Oldaker Run Picnic area. That's where we always have our July 4th District picnic. I told everyone that you and your family would be there, so they're looking forward to meeting you all.

"A couple of our recreation technicians are out today making sure things look good for this weekend. We get a lot of hiking, camping, fishing, and picnicking every July 4th holiday. Those two guys, Biggie Stone and Joe Slavens, are usually off on Tuesday and Wednesday during the summer, so that they can work on weekends. Next week, they'll also take off on Thursday as their "official" holiday since they have to work on Monday. But they'll plan their work to stop by and meet you at the picnic on Sunday."

"Come on outside for a minute," Vince said. "I'd like you to meet the family."

After introductions and a few minutes' worth of conversation, Stan told Vince it would be easiest to drive back out to the main entrance and park in the space beside the house just off the state highway. The Ranger's house was officially located fronting the highway, while the rest of the compound was setting back off the road 50 yards or so and had a different entrance.

It was all set in a traditional Forest Service "compound" that was common throughout the country at the more remote agency locations. In addition to the Ranger's house, there was the office, a house for the Assistant Ranger, a warehouse/work center that housed most of the District's tools and equipment, and a separate trailer that was used to house temporary summer help. On most work mornings the Ranger would always walk from the back of his house along a path just across a wide yard to the office to go to work.

The house itself was a very nice, large, two-story white home with green trim. It had a two-car garage and an out-building for mowers, tools, and other storage. The whole place appeared to have been well taken care of and all of the family, including Valerie, was eager to go inside and look around before they unpacked their vehicle.

Brian and Phil were excited when they found out they would each have their own separate bedrooms. The boys had always had to share a bedroom at their previous residences. Valerie had the largest of the three upstairs bedrooms, while Vince and Rita would have the master bedroom on the first floor. And surprise of surprises, there were two separate bathrooms upstairs, each with a bathtub/shower combination. That pleased Valerie to no end. She would claim one of those and the two boys could share the other. Downstairs there was a full bath off the master and a half-bath on the other side of the house.

As far as space went, this was the "roomiest" home the Taylor's had ever lived in. The kitchen was nice with great appliances, including a dishwasher and microwave, and there was room for a table and chairs at one end. The refrigerator was turned on, as was the electric and the water.

There was a large living room with a half wall separating it from a formal dining room off the kitchen. It was a great set-up, but it immediately got Rita wondering if they had enough furniture to fill up all the space. Oh well, she thought to herself, they needed to buy some new items anyway.

Stan had gotten permission from the Supervisor's Office to "rent" enough furniture for the Ranger and his family to use over the weekend. Jamison's friend, Ray Gifford, ran a grocery store and a furniture store in a nearby town. He often rented furniture and appliances to local families. He agreed to rent the Forest Service four beds with pillows and linens, a couch, a recliner, a TV, two living room chairs, and a kitchen/chair set for the weekend for $250; and that included delivery and pickup at the end of the Ranger's stay. What a deal! Kind of a special one for the Forest Service.

Jamison had told Vince that Gifford's Grocery was open until 7:00 p.m., so they would have to go down there and purchase what food and other essentials they would need for the next several days. Stan said that since they would be the guests of honor at the picnic on Sunday, they wouldn't have to worry about bringing anything to that event.

Stan also brought in towels, soap, shampoo, and wash cloths from his house for the Taylor's to use over the weekend. The Forest Service was purchasing a new washer and dryer for the residence because the old ones had been on their last leg. But those wouldn't be installed for a couple of more weeks. Stan also gave Vince a box of trash bags for the used towels and wash cloths and he would pick those up after they left. Same with any garbage bags they filled up.

All in all, it was very well thought out and Vince and Rita were extremely pleased.

The two boys had explored the house and were now out running around the yard. After Valerie's initial excitement about the large bedroom and her own bathroom, Rita found her out back sitting on the porch steps with a dejected look on her face.

"Why so glum, honey?" asked Rita. "Don't you like the house?"

"The house is fine, mom," replied Valerie, "but haven't you noticed we'll be living out in the boonies? I only saw a couple of houses nearby and one gas station up around the bend. And that's it! I probably won't have a friend living within 10 miles of this place," she said, as tears ran down her cheeks.

Rita put her arms around Valerie and said, "It's definitely out in the country, as compared to living in Ironton. But let's give it a chance. Please, let's just give it a chance."

The Taylor's spent Saturday driving around the area and exploring a little bit. They all agreed that this was one of the most beautiful and scenic areas they had ever seen. But it was definitely remote. There were a few country stores scattered around, as well as a few gas stations and clusters of homes here and there. All in all, Pocahontas County was sparsely populated.

The family drove the 20 or so miles down to the high school in Dunmore so that Valerie could see it. It was very nice and well kept; the only problem for Valerie was that she would be riding a bus back and forth to school every day – for the next two years! She was silent for most of the trip.

Vince and the two boys were excited about the mountains and streams for fishing, hunting, hiking, and just exploring in general. Rita tried her best to console Valerie and point out all of the positive things she could think of. But Valerie was pretty depressed and didn't say much during the day.

Later that evening, the family drove to Durbin, about three miles west of Bartow. Durbin was a bigger town than Bartow and the family had a meal at a local restaurant there. They also decided to attend church in Durbin on Sunday morning before heading to the picnic.

After getting back to Bartow on Saturday evening, Vince went over to the office and the warehouse area to check things out. It was a typical Forest Service layout and everything seemed to be well organized. The Assistant Ranger, Lonnie Bice, and his family, who were originally from Wisconsin, were not home. They had taken a short Friday-Saturday trip to Charleston but were planning to be back in Bartow for the District picnic on Sunday. Vince had talked on the phone with Bice after he learned he would be the next

Ranger in Bartow. They had a nice chat about the District and everything that was going on and it seemed like they would get along very well.

* * * * * * *

After church on Sunday and meeting several people from the area, the Taylor's returned to Bartow and changed into casual clothes for the picnic, which was scheduled to begin at 1:00 p.m. The distance to the Forest Service picnic area at Oldaker Run was only about five miles and within 15 minutes the Taylor's arrived. There were quite a few vehicles in the parking lot and Vince could see a group of men grilling hot dogs and hamburgers. Several women were placing various side dishes on tables and people were already playing volleyball and croquet. There were quite a few kids, who seemed to be about the same ages as Brian and Phil, running around.

As the Taylor's walked over to the area where most of the people had gathered, Stan Jamison came over to meet them and introduce them to everyone.

What a friendly group, Rita thought, as she and Vince shook one hand after another. "It's going to be hard to remember everyone's name," Rita told Stan.

"Oh, don't worry about it," Stan said. "There aren't that many of them and before long you'll have it down pat."

"Let's have the new Ranger say a few words," Stan told the group, which probably numbered 30 or more people.

"Well, we're happy to be coming here," Vince told them. "I've heard great things about this District from Stan, and also the Forest Supervisor, and I look forward to working with all of you to continue the fine work that you've always done here. We'll be back for good the first week in August. That's about all I have for now."

After a short prayer by Stan, it was time to eat.

Vince had noticed that Valerie was very quiet and had even rolled her eyes a couple of time when he was addressing the group.

"Come on Val," he told her. "Let's enjoy the day, have some good food, and meet a few people. I saw a volleyball game going on when we first pulled in. Maybe you can show them how it's done in Ironton."

Valerie smiled a little at that last remark, but did not seem at all happy to be there.

Vince mingled among the crowd, while his family sat at a picnic table to eat. Soon the two boys were finished eating and were running around the area with three or four other young boys they had just met. They were going to fit in just fine, Vince thought. Several of the wives came over to talk more with Rita. Valerie just sat and ate with her head down most of the time.

Vince had a chance to finally meet and talk with Lonnie Bice and also meet Biggie Stone and Joe Slavens, who were out patrolling the recreation areas over the July 4th weekend. They told Vince that there were a lot of people out picnicking, fishing, hiking and so forth, but there were no problems with anything they had seen. Vince was really impressed with all of the employees he had met and was so happy that they all seemed glad to have a new Ranger on board, too.

Vince began talking with one of the lead Forestry Technicians, Rick Daigle, and soon learned that they had several Forest Service friends in common. Rick was originally from upstate New York and had attended the New York State Ranger School, a very highly thought of training ground for forestry technicians. Rick had worked on several special assignments throughout the Forest Service Region 9 and that is where he had met some employees that Vince also knew. Rick had come to Bartow and the Monongahela National Forest right out of school, met and married a local girl, and planned to stay here permanently. He had a son who was going to be a junior in high school and a daughter in the seventh grade.

After Valerie finished eating, she got up to walk over and check out the volleyball group, which had just begun to choose sides for a friendly game. One of the older boys saw her and said she could be on his team.

"Hi, my name is Steve. Steve Daigle," he said, as he walked toward her. "You're on our team. I guess you're Valerie, the new Ranger's daughter. Have you played much volleyball?"

"A little bit," Valerie said, not wanting to let them know she was probably the best player at her high school in Ironton.

"Well, we'll keep you straight on the rules," said Steve. "We don't take it too seriously, but we do try to win. Just ask, if you have any questions," he said, as he smiled at Valerie.

What a good-looking boy, Valerie thought to herself. And he seems very nice, too.

There were enough players for six on a side. "We'll serve first," Steve told the group.

Steve couldn't help but notice how cute Valerie was, and very athletic looking, too.

"I'll serve," Steve said to Valerie. "Watch me and you can see how it's done. Then, you'll know what to do when it's your turn to serve."

Steve proceeded to serve by hitting the volleyball in the traditional underhanded manner. Their opponents failed to return the ball, so Steve's team scored the first point. "You get three tries to hit the ball back over the net," Steve explained to Valerie. "Then the other team gets three hits to get it back over. You can't catch the ball or "carry" it, either. You have to let it hit cleanly off your hands. Watch me, if you're not sure what I'm talking about."

Steve's next serve went out of bounds, so the other team then served. Their serve was fielded by Steve and he hit it up into the air near Valerie. She proceeded to jump up and smash it to the other side for a winning point.

"Great shot," yelled Steve. "I think you'll be pretty good once you practice this game some. Now, it's your turn to serve. Remember how I did it."

Valerie didn't want to show off, so she didn't do a jump serve, which she had learned when she played for Ironton High School. But she did do an overhand serve with considerable speed to it. Needless to say, it hit the ground for a winning point. So did Valerie's next three serves, with their opponents failing to even get the ball into the air. When Valerie finally hit a bad serve into the net, her side was ahead 12 – 2.

Steve didn't say much and as the game continued, Valerie had a few more kills and they eventually won the game 21 – 5.

"Wow," Steve said to Valerie. "Where did you learn to play like that?"

"I watched quite a bit of volleyball growing up," Valerie explained. "I guess I'm a fast learner. Plus, I played a little bit in high school last year in Ohio."

"Well, I can tell you one thing," said Steve. "Once you learn all the rules and everything, you'll be one of the best players at our school. Maybe the best. I sure hope you go out for the team here."

"I probably will," said Valerie. "Hopefully, I can make the team."

"From what I saw, you definitely will. Wanna go get another hot dog or some dessert or something?" Steve asked.

"Sure," Valerie replied. "And maybe you can tell me all about Pocahontas County High School."

Steve had another hot dog and a piece of chocolate cake, while Valerie ate a slice of homemade apple pie. He told her all about the high school and some of the teachers. He also told her that he played both football and basketball for the Warriors, which was the school's nickname.

Valerie asked about a track team and Steve said that they had one, but it was only a couple of years old and it was still growing. The head track coach was the assistant football coach and he was trying to get more students interested in the track program.

"Do you think you'll run track, too?" Steve asked. "Maybe I should do that also. I'm a pretty fast runner and I'm sure coach could use me. Did you run track in Ohio?"

"Yes, I ran the 400, 800, and did the long jump. We had a good track team and I really like it," she said.

Valerie found out that Steve lived in Boyer, only about five miles from Bartow on the road toward the high school. She told him that she was kind of bummed out thinking about having to take the bus to school every day.

"Yeah, I know what you mean," Steve told her. "Luckily, my parents got me a good used car and I drove it to school every day last year. Hey, maybe you could ride with me to school, if it's all right with your parents."

"Wow, that would be great!" Valerie said. "Let's wait and bounce that off our parents after we move here full time in August. It can be our little secret until then. When do you start football practice, anyway?"

"I think it's the second week in August," said Steve. "I'll have to check on that soon."

"What position do you play?" asked Valerie.

"I'm a running back. I also play safety on defense and last year I was the back-up quarterback, too," Steve explained. "That was only because we didn't really have a good second-string quarterback, but this year coach said I won't have to do that. We have another quarterback who moved into the area from Virginia. Coach said he's supposed to be pretty good."

They talked some more about classes, going to college in a couple of years, and other classmates that they would have in the fall. It finally came out during their discussion that Valerie was really good in volleyball and that she had been one of the fastest runners in her area of Ohio in the 400-meter run.

"The coaches are going to be really glad you moved here," said Steve. "And I was just wondering, do you have a boyfriend in Ohio?"

"I used to," she said, "but we broke up a couple of months ago. Do you have a girlfriend?"

"Not anymore," Steve replied. "I've had one or two, but nothing serious and no one right now."

That's good, Valerie thought to herself. I kind of like this boy. He's easy to talk with and he's so-o-o good looking. I sure want to get to know him better when we move here.

Valerie and Steve finished eating and walked back over to the volleyball area. Soon, they were involved in another game, which, once again, was dominated by Valerie. Steve said he was going to come to every volleyball game to watch her play. And Valerie said she was going to come to the football games to watch him play.

Even though Valerie was still somewhat upset that they were having to move from Ironton to Bartow, she was really happy that they had come to the Forest Service picnic. And that she had met Steve. They exchanged phone numbers and planned to talk with one another a few times over the next month.

It didn't go unnoticed by Rita that Valerie had spent a lot of time at the picnic talking with Steve Daigle. Vince told Rita that Steve was the son of the lead Forestry Technician on the District.

On the ride back to the Forest Service house, Vince asked the kids if they had enjoyed the picnic.

"It was great," said Phil. "We made a lot of new friends and explored the area. The food was good, too."

"Phil ate four hot dogs," said Brian. "I told him that was too many."

"Mind your own business," Phil told Brian.

"Don't you boys start arguing," Rita said.

"When we went over to the creek," Brian said, "we saw a snake and also a big fish. One of our new friends said it was a trout. I can't wait until we get to go fishing here Dad."

"We will definitely have time to do that," Vince said. "There is supposed to be some great trout fishing in this area, and some smallmouth bass streams, too. Plus, I'm looking forward to doing some deer hunting. Rick Daigle and Lonnie Bice have both already invited me to go deer hunting with them next fall."

"Speaking of Rick Daigle," Rita said, "was that his son I saw you spending so much time with today, Valerie?"

"Yes, it was, mom. You know it was," Valerie replied.

"Well, he seems like a nice young man," said Rita. "I met his mother today, too. They appear to be a very nice family. Do you think you and Steve will become good friends?"

"Who knows, mom, who knows?" said Valerie. But in her mind, she was thinking, I sure hope so.

Vince and Rita exchanged glances and each had a slight smile on their face.

*   *   *   *   *   *   *

The Taylor's spent the rest of the day in what was going to become their new home in a month. They ate leftovers that the District wives had put together for them to bring back from the picnic. Vince and the boys walked around the Forest Service grounds and checked things out a little closer. There was a nice sized garden space left from the previous Ranger and Vince figured he would definitely make good use of that next Spring. He might even plant a few items in August, after they moved, to be harvested later in the fall.

This was going to be a wonderful place to live, Vince thought. He just hoped that the family could get used to having only a few neighbors living close by. Especially Valerie. He knew it could be a rough move for her, since she was all set to enter her junior year in high school.

On Monday morning the family got up and walked over to the Bice's, who had invited them over for a big sendoff breakfast – pancakes, eggs, bacon, toast, coffee, juice, and a big bowl of mixed fruit. Vince had more time to talk with Lonnie about the District and what projects would be upcoming after he got there in August.

Rita was able to spend time getting to know Lonnie's wife, Mary, and their two daughters - Susan, age six, and Stephanie, age 3. Valerie was sitting with them and Mary inquired about whether she did any babysitting.

58

"I have done some babysitting over the past couple of years in Ironton," Valerie said. "I'd be glad to babysit for the two girls. Sometimes I get stuck babysitting with my two brothers and all they want to do is pick and pester one another – or me. The two girls would be a welcome change."

In a short while the Taylor's said their goodbye's and thanked the Bice's for a nice breakfast. Vince told Lonnie that he would call him a couple of times before August 3rd and that he was looking forward to working with him. They headed back over to the house, tidied things up, and packed the car. Vince left everything the way Stan Jamison had asked, locked up, and put the door key under the flowerpot on the back porch. Stan said he would come up later in the afternoon, get the key, and take care of everything.

They were on the road by 10:30 and hoped to get back to Ironton by late afternoon. All in all, it had been a very nice trip. Vince hoped it would make their move and transition to living in Bartow easier once they got back over there next month.

*   *   *   *   *   *   *

The rest of July was taken up with saying their goodbye's to friends in Ironton; arranging for the movers; and attending their going-away party. They rented a small U-Haul trailer to take some things that they did not want the movers to handle.

The two boys couldn't wait to move and get into their new home in Bartow. Valerie was a little less enthusiastic. The finality of the move was finally getting to her. She spent quite a bit of time with her two best friends, Janelle and Patti, who were still trying to get her to talk her parents into letting her stay in Ironton with one of them.

The one thing that kept Valerie's spirits up somewhat was that she and Steve had talked on the phone several times. He and his dad, along with Lonnie Bice, planned to come over and help the Taylor's get all of their belongings situated once the movers arrived in Bartow, which was scheduled for the Saturday before Vince was to begin his new job.

Steve said that he had talked with the volleyball coach and told her what a good player Valerie was. He said the coach was excited about that and would be in touch with them soon after they arrived in Bartow. Pre-season volleyball practice and tryouts, along with Steve's football practices, would begin about two weeks before classes started in late August.

Steve also told Valerie that he had talked with the track coach about Valerie and mentioned that she had run the 400- and 800-meter races in Ohio, and did the long jump, too. Valerie had told Steve that she had run a 400-meter race in just under 60 seconds and had an 800-meter time of about 2:20. The coach was excited and told Steve that both of those times were better than the current Pocahontas County High School records. She had also jumped just over 17-feet in the long jump, Steve had told the coach, and that, too, would be a new school record.

"I can't wait until you get here," Steve told Valerie on their last phone call. "We can go down to the school and I'll introduce you to the coaches and some of our classmates. I'll be at every one of your volleyball matches, unless the football team is out of town at a game or something. And I hope you can come to the football games, at least the home games. I should be the starting tailback and a safety on defense. And I've decided I'm going to run track next spring, too.

"By the way, have you asked your parents if it would be all right for you to ride to school with me?" Steve asked Valerie.

"Not yet," Valerie said, "but I don't think it will be a problem. I was planning to wait until we get over there to bring that up with them. And Steve, just so you know, I'm looking forward to getting to Pocahontas County and hopefully spending more time with you, too.

"This move was not something that I was initially looking forward to," Valerie continued, "but since meeting you and talking with you more on the phone, I have changed my mind. I appreciate you taking the time to talk with the coaches and offering to give me rides to school, too. You've been really great."

"I'll be counting the days until you get here," Steve had told her.

One evening, Rita asked Valerie if she had been talking with Steve on the phone some.

"I think you know the answer to that, mom" Valerie said. "He's very nice. I like him a lot."

Valerie told her mom about Steve telling the volleyball and track coaches about her. And that they were planning to go on some dates once they got over to Pocahontas County.

"Well, I think that's good," Rita said. "Just make sure to take things slow until you get to know him better."

"Mom, you know I will," replied Valerie.

*   *   *   *   *   *   *

Well, moving day came and before long everything was loaded and the Taylor's were saying goodbye to Ironton, Ohio and headed for Bartow, West Virginia. They would spend the night in Elkins and meet the movers the next morning at their new house.

On Saturday morning they arrived in Bartow ahead of the movers. There to meet them were Lonnie

Bice, Stan Jamison, Rick Daigle, and, of course, Steve.
Steve also brought his best friend, Joe Lambert, with
him to help out, too.

Steve wasted no time in coming over to say hello,
introduce Joe, and give Valerie a hug. "I'm sure glad
you're finally here," he told her. "I thought the day
would never come."

"Me, too," said a smiling Valerie. "It's so good to
see you again."

The moving truck arrived and Steve told Valerie
they could talk some more after they got everything
moved in.

As they walked over to where the truck was
backing in, Joe leaned over to Steve and said, "You were
right this time, buddy. She's a knockout. If she wasn't
your girl, I'd ask her out myself. But maybe I'd better
not," Joe said grinning.

"Good idea. Buddy," Steve said, not grinning at
all.

"Relax, Steve. I was just kidding," said Joe.

It took a couple of hours to unload everything
before Steve and Valerie had a chance to talk some
more. They tentatively planned for Steve to pick her up
on Tuesday morning and go down to the high school
and meet some of the teachers and coaches. Rita said

that was fine and that she would have Valerie take her paperwork with her to start the enrollment process for the new school. Rita would handle getting the two boys enrolled in their new school in Green Bank.

Mary Bice came over and offered to help Rita with getting things arranged in the house, especially the kitchen. They decided to do that the following afternoon.

Steve told Valerie that it would be his last free week before the football team started two weeks of pre-season practice. And he was pretty sure that was the same schedule for the volleyball team. Then, school would start the last week of the month.

Steve said that if their practice schedules worked out, he could drive Valerie to practice every day, too. Valerie's mother said that would be great, since she would be busy with the two boys and Vince would be busy learning about his new job. Rita said that on one of the days, she would take Valerie to the school herself, so that she could meet the principal and some of the teachers and coaches, as well as sign any papers that were necessary.

Valerie and Steve were both excited about the coming weeks and they discussed about going on a date once they got their schedules worked out. They would get a good start on that after they went to the school on Tuesday.

Steve picked up Valerie Tuesday morning and they drove down to the high school, where he introduced her to the principal, a few teachers, and the volleyball coach. They also talked with the assistant football coach, who would be coaching both the boys and the girls track teams in the spring.

Everyone was excited about Valerie coming to school there. The principal's secretary made copies of the information Valerie had brought with her from Ironton. She filled out some additional paperwork and got more information to take back home to her parents.

As it turned out, both the volleyball tryouts and the football practice would start the following Monday at 9:00 a.m. So, that would work perfectly for Steve and Valerie to go there together. The volleyball coach gave Valerie a practice schedule, a handout explaining the program and the coach's expectations, a game schedule for the fall season, and a sheet with miscellaneous information about what practice clothes to wear, and so on. The coach also mentioned that once she had heard about Valerie moving to Bartow, she had called her coach in Ironton to find out a little bit about her. And it was all very positive.

"We'll have to see how practices go, of course," the coach said, "but from what I hear, you'll be an important part of our team this fall. I'm certainly looking forward to having you on our team."

On the drive back to Bartow, Steve asked Valerie if they could go on a date before practices started the following Monday.

"That would be great," Valerie said enthusiastically. "I'll probably have to help mom around the house for a few days though."

"That's fine," said Steve. "I was thinking about Saturday anyway. Some of our friends are getting together for a cookout that evening before the football practices and the other pre-school meetings and activities begin. That way you could meet a lot of our classmates before school starts."

"Sounds good, Steve," said Valerie. "I'll bounce it off mom and dad to make sure they don't have anything planned, but I'm sure it will work out. You are sure being nice to me and helpful."

"Well, in case you haven't noticed," Steve said, "I like you. A lot."

"I like you a lot, too," Valerie said, as she was sure that she was blushing. This move might turn out to be one of the best things ever, Valerie thought to herself.

Steve picked up Valerie on Saturday evening and they drove down to Arbovale, where about 15 or 20 students were having a cookout in the side yard where one of Steve's football teammates lived.

Valerie certainly couldn't remember everyone's name, but they were all very nice and she was also able to meet two of her future volleyball teammates. When Steve took Valerie home that evening, they stayed out in his car and talked for quite a while. They discussed school, favorite classes, plans for after high school, and just generally got to know each other better.

"Well, I'd better head on home," Steve said, as he leaned over to hug Valerie and he gave her a kiss on the cheek.

Valerie was hoping for more and after she hugged Steve back, she kept her face close to his and told him what a great time she had that evening. Steve instinctively leaned in a planted a big kiss on Valerie's lips.

"I hope you were okay with that," he said. "I just couldn't help it. You're so pretty and I guess you could say that I'm falling for you."

Valerie giggled and said, "I'm falling for you, too," as she leaned in for a longer kiss this time. Then there was one more even longer kiss before Valerie said, "I think I'd better get inside now. I think I saw mom looking out the window."

"Sure," said Steve. "I don't want to get your parents mad at me. But I had fun this evening and I'm really, really glad you moved here."

"Me, too," said Valerie.

They agreed that Steve would pick her up Monday morning at 8:00 a.m. so that they could get to the school for their practices in plenty of time.

Valerie went inside and her mother was sitting on the couch. "You were sure outside in the driveway a long time," Rita said. "What was that all about?"

"We were talking about classes, sports, what kinds of things we both liked to do, and even talked about college a little bit," said Valerie. "Basically, just getting to know each other better. By the way, were you looking out the window at us?"

"Me?" Rita asked. "Would I ever do such a thing?" she said, smiling. "You two seem to be getting along very well. Just make sure you know what you're doing."

"We're fine," said Valerie. "By the way, I was just wondering how old you were when you and dad met and started dating?"

"We were in the 9th grade," Rita said. "My parents had just moved to the part of town where he went to school. I thought he was the cutest boy I had ever seen."

"Enough said," Valerie replied. "I'm two years older than you were then. And, oh mom, I think Steve is just about the cutest boy I've ever seen. Good night. I love you."

Valerie and Steve drove to practices together the next two weeks, except for one day when Rita took her, so that she could talk with the principal and some of the teachers. Steve and Valerie were basically pretty tired and worn out at the end of each day, but they did have more time to talk about things during their drives to and from school. On the Saturday before classes began, Steve invited Valerie to have dinner with his family. When he took her home later that evening, he asked Valerie if she would become his girlfriend and that they could officially become a couple before school started.

"Oh yes, yes, yes," Valerie said. "Nothing could make me happier. I've been thinking about that, too."

So, when classes began, all the buzz around school was that Steve Daigle and the new girl were dating. And Valerie and Steve loved hearing that; and telling their friends that, yes, it was true.

And although Steve was definitely known as one of the best athletes in school, everyone was talking about how good Valerie was in volleyball. With several other girls returning from last year's team, the coach was expecting to have a very good season.

* * * * * * *

Valerie and Steve continued to be a steady couple throughout the fall. The football team had an excellent season, losing only to East Hardy and Midland Trail. Their record qualified them for the post-season playoffs, where they unfortunately lost the first game to eventual state champion Williamstown. However, it was Pocahontas County's best season in quite a few years and several key players, including Steve Daigle, were returning next year. Steve made the Class A All-State team and was already drawing attention from several college coaches.

The volleyball team had a great year, also. In fact, it was their best season ever, losing only two early season matches before the post-season tournaments. They, too, would have several key players returning the following year. The Lady Warriors won their sectional tournament, but failed to advance past the regionals. They had been hoping for a state tournament berth, but after the sting of their regional loss had worn off, they all realized what a great year they had experienced.

Valerie had quickly become known as the best player on the team and, along with a couple of other excellent players, Pocahontas County volleyball was definitely a team on the rise.

College contact letters were already pouring in for Valerie, from schools in Pennsylvania, Virginia, Ohio, and West Virginia. And she still had one year left in high school. One school in particular, Fairmont State

University in Fairmont, WV, was especially aggressive in pursuing Valerie. That college had a very good volleyball program and was part of the NCAA Division II Mountain East Conference (MEC).

Valerie and her parents had taken a weekend trip up to Fairmont to visit the school and talk with the coaches. It was only a little over two hours from Bartow, so that was certainly a plus. Steve and Valerie had become almost inseparable, so, of course, he went with them. Fairmont was also one of the schools that had been in contact with Steve for football.

The Taylor's were all very impressed with Fairmont State and the volleyball program. Valerie had hit it off instantly with the coaches. And although they couldn't officially offer a scholarship to Valerie until next year, they all but told her to expect that. And from what the coaches said, it would likely be a full scholarship offer. That was good news for the Taylor's.

Since Fairmont was not very far from Bartow, The Taylor's could see most of Valerie's games. Also, 10 of the 12 schools in the MEC were located in West Virginia, so they would be able to travel to many of those "away" matches, too. One of the MEC colleges was located in Ohio and one was in Maryland.

As far as what she would study in college, Valerie had always liked biology, ecology, and environmental science. She could teach that in high school and maybe coach volleyball; or she could even work on a graduate degree in one of those fields. A career with a state or national park or forest might be interesting, too, she had always thought. But she would have plenty of time to decide on that.

Steve was a real whiz with computers and he loved keeping up with all of the latest technology. He told Valerie that he would likely major in computer science in college.

Luckily, if they attended Fairmont State, that school had strong programs in both of the fields they were interested in.

Steve and Valerie had gone to the Homecoming Dance together that fall and were already planning to attend the Sweetheart Dance in February and, yes, the Junior-Senior Prom in the spring. As the year wore on, Valerie and Steve became closer and closer and each could see them eventually getting married and having a life together.

They still had their senior year of high school ahead of them, as well as college, and many experiences to share and memories to make. Steve, especially, wanted to have a good senior year in football, so that he could earn a scholarship offer from Fairmont State. It was pretty evident that that was the school Valerie would attend.

The Taylor's had initially been a little concerned about moving from Ironton, Ohio to a more remote and rural area of West Virginia. But the family was settling in and beginning to enjoy Pocahontas County. Valerie, obviously, had fit right in with the high school and, yes, with a new boyfriend. The two boys enjoyed all of the fishing, hiking, and running around in the forests of the area with their dad. They had also made several friends at school and had several sleepovers with them.

Rita had become close friends with a couple of the Forest Service wives and had also gotten to know several women through the Homemakers Club. Vince thoroughly enjoyed his work as District Ranger at Bartow. He had an excellent staff and crew of workers, as well as a very good boss, the Forest Supervisor, in Elkins. There was a good variety of work with various projects in wildlife management, outdoor recreation, soil & water improvement projects, and timber management. They had also agreed to host a summer youth program of high school kids who would help primarily in hiking trail maintenance and various other recreation programs.

All in all, the move to Pocahontas County had been very positive for the Taylor's.

*   *   *   *   *   *   *

One evening in January, when they were getting ready to attend one of the high school basketball games, where Steve was probably the team's best player, Valerie said to her mom, "I think this move to Bartow is the best thing that has ever happened to us."

"Wow," said Rita. "I seem to remember that you didn't even want to come here. You were begging to stay in Ironton with either Janelle or Patti's family. What's caused you to change your mind so completely?" Rita said to Valerie with a slight grin on her face.

"I think you know," replied Valerie, also with a smile toward her mother. "Steve is just about the best thing that has ever happened to me. I know I'm still kind of young, mom, but I love him!"

"I know you do, sweetheart," said Rita. "He's a fine young man and I'm very happy for you."

Chapter 3

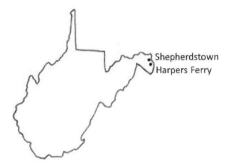

Shepherdstown
Harpers Ferry

HARPERS FERRY HOLIDAY

Lee Maxey decided to take a day off from studying and from his two summer on-line classes through Shepherd University. In the spring he had just finished his sophomore year in the pre-dental program at the college, which was located in Shepherdstown, West Virginia. His advisor had told him that taking the two summer courses would help make him eligible to apply for dental school at West Virginia University after completing his third year at Shepherd.

His course work in the pre-dental program was heavy toward chemistry, biology, physics, and math classes, but he loved those courses and he had a high grade point average. In fact, Lee had made only one B in college so far, and he planned to keep it that way. And the B had been in, you guessed it, English, which was not his favorite subject.

If he didn't get accepted at WVU after his junior year at Shepherd, although his advisor thought he likely would, then plan B would be to return to Shepherd and complete his Bachelor of Science degree in either chemistry or biology. Then, he would re-apply for dental school at WVU, as well as possibly the University of Pittsburgh and the University of Maryland at Baltimore.

Both of those other colleges had good dental schools. He wasn't thrilled with potentially attending school in Baltimore, but he would if he had to. Lee had attended a couple of Baltimore Orioles baseball games with his friends over the years and that was kind of fun. But besides those games at Camden Yards and some nice attractions around the Inner Harbor, he could take or leave the rest of the city. The traffic was terrible and the crime rate was high. Even if you avoided the worst parts of the city, it seemed like someone was always getting robbed or shot just about anywhere in Baltimore.

Of course, Lee's dad, Will, had graduated from Pitt, so that wouldn't be too bad. But Lee preferred WVU and would keep his fingers crossed for that. He had been to Morgantown several times over the years and he really liked that area better than Pittsburgh. Will had grown up in the small town of Fairchance, Pennsylvania just north of the West Virginia border near Morgantown. As a kid growing up, Lee had often spent time with his grandparents in Fairchance. Lee's parents eventually settled in Hagerstown, Maryland, where his dad now worked and where Lee had grown up.

But today Lee was taking a day off from his studies. He was heading from his parents' home in Hagerstown over to Harpers Ferry National Park in West Virginia. It would be about a 45 minute drive.

Lee had worked at the park last summer. Sometimes they had even sent his crew to work at the Appalachian Trail (AT) Visitor Center in Harpers Ferry or to do some trail maintenance on the AT itself. He still had friends at the park, as well as the AT Visitor Center, and he hoped to visit with them today. Then he planned to walk around the town some and probably get a bite to eat in one of the quaint local restaurants. Harpers Ferry was certainly an interesting town, with lots of history, small stores, and restaurants.

After stopping at the park's visitor center and talking with a couple of his friends, Lee walked over to the AT Visitor Center. There was no one there today that he knew, but he did strike up an interesting conversation with an attractive young lady who was working as an information assistant. He learned that her name was Jenny Lewis. She told him that she was a college student who had grown up in Harpers Ferry, attended Jefferson High School, and was living with her parents for the summer before going back to school.

"I worked here last summer," Lee said. "I really enjoyed it. You look familiar, but I don't remember seeing you here. And I certainly would have remembered that," he said with a grin.

"No, I wasn't here last summer," said Jenny. "For the previous two summers I worked at the Antietam National Battlefield over in Maryland. It's only about a half hour from here."

"I know exactly where it is," explained Lee. "I live in Hagerstown, which isn't even ½ an hour from Antietam. I've been there many times. Plus, my mother grew up in Sharpsburg, which is only a mile or so south of the battlefield."

"Maybe I saw you in the visitor center at Antietam last summer or the summer before that," Lee continued. "You sure do look familiar."

"So do you," Jenny said. "How many summers did you work here in Harpers Ferry?"

"Just the one," said Lee. "The summer before that, which was right after I graduated from high school, I worked in, what else, but fast food. I got tired of that, which led me to apply for the summer job here last year. I really enjoyed it, but this summer I'm taking two on-line courses from college, so I'm not working; except a couple of evenings a week cleaning up at a bakery in town. My mother knows the lady who runs the bakery and she got that lined up for me. It's only a few hours a week, but it does give me a little bit of spending money.

"Scholarships are paying most of my college costs," continued Lee, "so my parents are okay with me concentrating this summer on my coursework. If I keep up my grade point average this coming year, I hope to get accepted into the dental program at WVU, which is another four years."

"Wow," said Jenny. "That's great. Are either of your parents dentists?"

"No," Lee said, "but I have an uncle who is a dentist in Uniontown, Pennsylvania. He's my father's younger brother. Since Uniontown is so close to Morgantown, if things work out for me, I should be able to help him some in his practice, as I get further along in my studies at WVU."

"Sounds like you have a definite plan," Jenny said. "By the way, where are you attending college now?"

"I go to Shepherd University, not far from here," Lee answered. "I'm sure you've heard of it."

"Heard of it!" Jenny exclaimed. "That's where I go, too."

"No kidding?" Lee asked. "Maybe that's where I've seen you because you sure do look familiar."

"I know," Jenny laughed. "You've said that a couple of times already."

"Sorry that I keep repeating myself," said Lee. "I guess since we have over 4,000 students at Shepherd it would be hard to remember everyone that goes to school there. But you sure do look familiar; woops, sorry," Lee said, as they both laughed.

Jenny went on to tell Lee that she would be a senior at Shepherd in the fall and that she was majoring in communications. She was actually considering going to WVU, too, and working on her master's degree. She wanted to eventually work in journalism or public relations in some capacity, but probably not for a government agency. If she could work at a newspaper or for a news organization for a few years and then possibly go into freelance work, that would be her preferred route. She got very good grades in her creative writing courses. Jenny's advisors told her that a graduate degree in journalism would be of great benefit in the highly competitive journalism field. And Morgantown was only about three hours away from her home in Harpers Ferry.

"Why wouldn't you want to work for a government agency, like at one of these visitor centers or something," asked Lee.

"I guess it would be all right," answered Jenny, "especially if I couldn't find work in those other areas that I mentioned. But my mother is a Public Affairs Officer (PAO) for the National Park Service and I see how they pull her around for multiple tasks and at numerous locations. I don't think I would like that."

Jenny went on to explain that her mother, Paula Lewis, did help her get the summer jobs where she had worked the past three summers, but that her mom was on the road a lot. Maybe it was just because she was in a shared job position supporting several National Park Service (NPS) locations.

Officially, her mother was stationed at the Antietam site, but spent quite a bit of time traveling to other Park Service locations to do public affairs work, too. In addition to Antietam, she did public affairs work for NPS facilities at Harpers Ferry, Manassas National Battlefield, the C&O Canal, and, of course the Appalachian Trail. From time to time she also did work at the Gettysburg National Military Park and the Shenandoah National Park. She even got pulled in to the national office in Washington, D.C. for special assignments on occasion. That was way too much travel as far as Jenny was concerned.

Paula Lewis wrote news releases; helped design brochures and handouts; posted information to web sites; corresponded with numerous media outlets via Facebook and Twitter; drafted speeches for her superiors; wrote script for TV and radio ads; gave interviews; took journalists on field trips, and more. It was definitely an interesting job, but Jenny thought that the workload was way too heavy.

Until recent years her mother had also had one or two assignments each year to serve as a Fire Information Officer on western forest fires, where she wrote press releases, talked with the media, answered phone calls, and things like that. But her current workload was so heavy that she couldn't afford to be gone for several weeks each summer, so she had to give that up, Jenny explained.

"That's very interesting," said Lee, "but I can see where the travel would get to be a bit much. And by the way my dad, Will, who got a degree in business management from Pitt, spent two summers with a Forest Service fire crew in Idaho while he was still in college. He said they never got very close to the worst forest fires. That was left up to the hot shot crews and the more experienced firefighters. His crew mostly did mop-up work after the fires were controlled, making sure there were no smoldering stumps or smoking snags or things like that, which could start another forest fire if left burning. He always told me that the work was interesting and exciting."

"I've heard my mother talk about all of those kinds of things. Seems like we have a lot in common," said Jenny.

"Yes, it sure does," Lee agreed. "I know you're busy and I need to leave you alone so that you can get back to work. But would you like to meet for lunch sometime and talk further? Maybe over in Shepherdstown, since that would be halfway between where we both live this summer. How about at the Moon Dog Café? Do you know where that is?"

"I sure do," answered Jenny. "It's a favorite with me and my friends."

"Great," said Lee. "What days are you off from work?"

"I have to work every weekend," replied Jenny, "but I'm off on Tuesdays and Wednesdays."

"Then, how about next Tuesday at the Moon Dog in Shepherdstown around noon or 12:30?" asked Lee. "Will that work for you? I need to swing by and talk with one of my professors that morning anyway, but that won't take more than an hour. I'll meet you at the Moon Dog Café at 12:30 p.m."

"I'll be there. See you then," said Jenny.

Man, what luck to meet her, Lee thought as he left the visitor center. I can't wait until next Tuesday.

*   *   *   *   *   *   *

Late morning, on the following Tuesday, Lee stopped by the biology building at Shepherd to talk with his advisor about the two summer courses he was taking and to confirm his schedule for the next two semesters. They wanted to make sure that they hadn't overlooked something and that everything would be in proper order for him to apply for the early admission dental school program at WVU. Lee's advisor told him that based upon his past experience with the early admissions at WVU, he stood an excellent chance.

So, Lee was in a very good mood as he headed over to the Moon Dog Café. And he was so looking forward to seeing Jenny Lewis again and getting to know her better.

It was almost 12:30 when Lee arrived and there was Jenny, sitting at a small table over in one corner of the café. "Sorry if I'm a little bit late," said Lee. "But I had a good talk with my professor. He thinks I stand an excellent chance of getting early admittance to the WVU dental program."

"That's great," said Jenny. "I've decided to definitely apply to the WVU master's degree program in journalism after the fall semester here at Shepherd. My grades are very good, so my advisor said she is almost certain that I'll get accepted. I should hear back from WVU early in the spring semester. So, hopefully we'll both be in Morgantown a year from now."

"Well, it's good news all the way around. What are you going to have for lunch? My treat," Lee said.

"I'm a creature of habit, so I usually order a BLT sandwich on wheat and some sweet potato fries," Jenny said. "I only had a cup of yogurt for breakfast, so I'm kind of hungry."

"A BLT sounds tasty," said Lee. "I had a big breakfast this morning, though, so I think I'll go with a salad – the grilled chicken and avocado salad."

The waitress came over and took their order and asked them if they wanted an appetizer. "Sure; let's get some chips and salsa" Lee told the waitress.

"That's good," said Jenny. "They always have the best homemade salsa here."

While they waited on their lunch to arrive, they continued their conversation from the previous week, eating a few chips and salsa as they talked. "So, you said you grew up in Harpers Ferry," Lee said.

"Yes, I did," Jenny replied. "Just on the outskirts of town. Mom grew up in Harpers Ferry, too; and my dad, whose name is Matt, was raised on a 300-acre farm north of there in the Bakerton area. His folks grew corn, soybeans, and had some hay fields, also. At one time they had a few head of cattle, but they eventually gave that up. The farm has been in dad's family for well over 100 years. His older sister, Nora, and her husband live there now and run the farm. They have a son who wants to continue operating the farm in the future, so we're happy that it will stay in the family."

"So, then your parents went to school together?" Lee asked.

"Well, sort of, but not really," said Jenny. "Same school, but a few years apart. Dad is several years older than mom and he had already graduated before she was in high school. By then, he was working on a degree in Economics at WVU. They didn't even know each other until well after he had graduated from college."

"Wow, that's amazing," commented Lee. "How did they meet then?"

"It's kind of a funny story," Jenny went on to explain. "After graduating from college, dad took a trainee position in the business management field with the U.S. Forest Service in Heber City, Utah. An advisor at WVU had seen that job opening on a posting that came through his office. Dad was fortunate to get that trainee position because they taught him about purchasing, personnel management, accounting, property management, tech support, and just about everything involved in the business management area of the Forest Service. A few years ago, we visited Heber City when we took a western vacation and it's a beautiful area east of Salt Lake City in the Uinta National Forest.

"After two years they transferred him to the Kaibab National Forest in Williams, Arizona," continued Jenny. "A few years later he changed agencies and applied for a position in Administration at the Rocky Mountain National Park in Estes Park, Colorado. That's an hour and a half or so north of Denver. And who should he meet there, but my mother, who was working as a summer student in Public Affairs. It was the summer before her senior year at WVU. When they found out that they were both from Jefferson County, West Virginia, they couldn't believe it."

"That sure was a coincidence," said Lee. "So they didn't even know each other back home?"

"No, although during their conversations she learned that he had known mom's older sister in high school," she said. "Mom and dad then went on a few dates and stayed in touch over the next year. Dad even went out with her a couple of times when he came back east for holiday visits. After her graduation from WVU and because of how well she had done in her job the previous summer, the Park Service offered her a position in Public Affairs in their Regional office in Denver. To make a long story short, dad transferred to the Regional Office, too; they got married; and they worked there for 10 years. My older sister, Laura, and I were both born in Denver."

"My goodness, when did you come back to Harpers Ferry?" asked Lee.

"Well, later on both of my parents wanted to get back closer to home," explained Jenny. "So dad took an assignment to the Washington, D.C. business office of the Department of the Interior, which includes the National Park Service. Mom was lucky in that there was also an opening in the Philadelphia Region of the Park Service. But it was assigned as a shared position located in Antietam and assisting those other locations that I mentioned to you the other day. They decided to settle down in the Harpers Ferry area, where they had both grown up. It's close to mom's primary office in Antietam, but dad has to drive a little over an hour to work each way. He hates that, but he can retire in a couple of years. He's got it figured out to the exact day. Lately, they have allowed him to work four ten-hour days each week and two of those are from home. Most of what he does is on a computer anyway and every so often they have conference calls."

"I can only imagine how difficult that commute must be," Lee said. "Thank goodness he has it down to just two days a week. But I know that there are quite a few people from the eastern panhandle in West Virginia who commute to D.C. or Baltimore for work. How long before your mother can retire?" he asked.

"I think it's something like seven or eight years," Jenny replied. "She's getting burned out with her job, so I think she will retire at the earliest opportunity."

By then, their lunch had arrived. "They have the best BLT sandwiches," Jenny said. "And I love these sweet potato fries."

"This salad is great, too," said Lee. "We'll have to make this our regular meeting place. That is, if you want to keep meeting me. And I sure hope that is the case."

"Sure would," replied Jenny. "And why do you keep staring at me?"

"Well, for one thing, you are very pretty. But I keep wondering where I've seen you before. You sure do look familiar," Lee said, forgetting that he kept repeating this statement.

"I haven't heard you say that before," said Jenny, as they both laughed and laughed.

"I'll try my best to not say that again," Lee smiled.

"We've heard enough about me and my family," Jenny continued. "How about your family? You said your dad helped fight forest fires out west when he was young, but I guess he didn't stay working in the natural resource field?"

"No, just the two summer jobs," explained Lee. "After he graduated from college, he got offered an entry level position with the City of Hagerstown, Maryland. He's been there ever since. He eventually became the head of business management and personnel, but he now serves as the Executive Assistant to the Mayor.

"My mother, Ann, is an English teacher at Boonsboro High School. I attended North Hagerstown High School," Lee continued. "I think I mentioned the other day that mom grew up in Sharpsburg. She got her teaching degree at Shepherd, which, I guess, is what led me to attend here. It's kind of funny because English is not my favorite subject; I get A's in just about everything, but B's in English. It's a running joke around our house."

The couple finished eating and then walked around Shepherdstown for a while before deciding it was time for them to return home. "I actually have to go over to the bakery for a few hours tonight to help clean up the place. But I've had a great time this afternoon," Lee said.

"Me, too," said Jenny. "I've really enjoyed it."

"We'll have to do this again before school starts," suggested Lee. "And if our schedules work out, maybe from time to time during the school year."

"That would be so nice," Jenny replied.

"Well, goodbye for now," Lee said as he gave Jenny a short hug. "I'll call you in a few days, if that's all right."

"It's certainly all right. I can't wait," Jenny said. "Be safe, and drive carefully, okay?"

"You too," he answered.

*   *   *   *   *   *   *

Lee and Jenny continued to meet for lunches during the fall semester at Shepherd. They often ate at the Moon Dog Café, as well as at the Student Center, where they occasionally also went bowling or played pool. And wouldn't you know it, Jenny was good. Lee usually beat Jenny at bowling, but not by much. However, when they played 8-ball on the pool tables, more often than not, Jenny came out the winner. That girl could shoot some pool! And Lee wondered how she got so good. Finally, she told him.

"We've had a pool table in our basement at home for years," Jenny admitted. "My dad is one of the best pool players you'll ever see. He's even been involved in a few tournaments in Pennsylvania and Maryland. He began teaching me some of the basics and I really liked it. So, I started to practice a lot on my own and to play more against my dad as I got better. I can beat him every once in a while. Really, it's just all about seeing the angles. I guess I'm a better than average pool shot."

"How did your dad get so good at pool?" Lee asked. "Are there pool halls in Harpers Ferry?"

"I think there used to be some in a bar around here, but he quit going there or they closed it or something," said Jenny. "But he goes over to Charles Town to shoot pool with some guys he knows. It's close, not even 10 miles from Harpers Ferry.

"But he told me that where he really learned to shoot pool was when he was in college in Morgantown," Jenny continued. "There were pool tables on campus at the student union where he and his friends played; and a couple of places downtown where they went to play, too. He said that he would watch guys play for money at the downtown pool halls. Guys would come from Pittsburgh and Wheeling to play in local tournaments for money and dad said that they were really good. He learned a lot by just watching them – the strategies and playing position with the cue ball, and so on."

"Well, if we both go to WVU next year and we ever need extra money, maybe you can enter a few local tournaments," Lee said, as he smiled at Jenny.

"I don't know if I'm that good or not," Jenny said, "but I do like to play pool."

Lee and Jenny were becoming a well-known couple on campus. Their friends would even kid them about how serious they seemed to be getting. But they were so compatible with things that it was easy to see that this could end up being a long-term relationship.

They attended one play at the Shepherd campus theater in the fall and they went to two football games – one against Slippery Rock and one against West Chester. Shepherd won both games; they usually had a very good football team. During the winter months they planned on attending some of the Rams' basketball games, too.

Lee and Jenny were hoping that things could continue for them at WVU the next year. Jenny's advisor had talked with the folks at the journalism school in Morgantown, which was actually called the Reed College of Media at WVU. Based upon her grade point average, and by getting early grade reports from her current professors at Shepherd, they learned that Jenny could send in her application for graduate school right after Thanksgiving.

That was great news for Jenny. With a little luck she would hear something back in January or early February and she could begin making firm plans for next year. She had learned that there were five or six specialty areas she could focus on for a master's degree at WVU and complete any one of them in a year, since she would be coming with a four-year degree in hand.

But if she wanted to spend two-years in grad school, Jenny could come out with twin MS degrees in Journalism and also in Integrated Marketing Communications.

In the journalism program she could take further courses in reporting, creative writing, and developing feature stories, as well as other traditional journalism areas. In the integrated marketing curriculum, she would learn more about public relations, community outreach, advertising, and marketing. Combining the two areas of study would offer Jenny a much broader opportunity for jobs. And, of course, each specialty area had a significant focus on the electronic and digital world.

Jenny was getting excited about her future, especially if Lee got accepted into the dental program at WVU and could be there with her.

Lee's advisor had been in contact with the folks at the WVU dental school and, unfortunately, they would not accept his application until later in the spring semester. That was a bummer, as far as Lee was concerned, but his advisors told him that they would sure be surprised if he didn't get accepted into the WVU dental program.

* * * * * * *

Neither Lee nor Jenny had met each other's parents yet, although they had both told them about this great person they were dating at Shepherd. Over lunch one day at the Moon Dog, several weeks after the fall semester had begun, Lee asked Jenny if she would mind having Thanksgiving dinner at the Maxey home, if he would agree to spend a day over Christmas with the Lewis' in Harpers Ferry. Jenny thought that was a fine plan, but, of course, they would have to clear it with their families first.

The Maxey's were excited about meeting Jenny and eagerly agreed to invite her for Thanksgiving. They had heard so much about her from Lee. Ann Maxey always prepared a big Thanksgiving meal with turkey and all of the traditional trimmings, as well as a small ham on the side.

Lee told Jenny that his older sister, Rita, who was also a high school English teacher in Frostburg, Maryland, and her husband would be joining them for Thanksgiving. Rita's husband, Dusty Jones, was the lacrosse coach at Frostburg State University, where he had been a star for the team several years ago. It was about an 80 mile drive from Frostburg to Hagerstown.

Since lacrosse was a spring sport at Frostburg, Dusty also taught two courses each fall in the college of education – one in sports management for prospective high school teacher/coaches and another in the philosophy of sports. Dusty had been an all-state lacrosse player in high school in Salisbury, on Maryland's eastern shore, but had come to love living in the mountains of western Maryland.

Matt and Paula Lewis were also eager to meet Jenny's boyfriend, Lee, and after talking about it, everyone decided the best day would be the day after Christmas, which was on a Friday. Matt and Paula were both taking a couple of weeks' vacation over the holidays and Jenny's aunt and uncle, as well as Jenny's sister, would be joining them, too. Her aunt and uncle had other plans for Christmas Eve and Christmas Day, so the day after Christmas worked best for them.

Jenny hadn't talked too much about her older sister, but Lee would meet her and get to know her over the holidays. He knew that her name was Laura, she was a nurse, not married, and was working down in Charleston. Jenny said she had attended WVU for two years before transferring to Marshall to complete her nursing degree.

Lee was hoping that he could also talk Jenny's dad into a few games of pool and perhaps get a few lessons from him while he was at it.

"I doubt if you'll have to talk dad into it," Jenny told Lee after he mentioned that to her. "If someone mentions they'd like to shoot some pool, dad is already halfway downstairs to the table," she laughed. "He loves it."

"Sounds like it's all going to work out then," said Lee. "My parents' house in Hagerstown for Thanksgiving and then to your folks' house over Christmas for a 'Harpers Ferry Holiday'."

"I can't wait," said Jenny.

"Me neither," said Lee.

*   *   *   *   *   *   *

Even though Lee and Jenny continued to see each other as often as possible during the fall semester, they also spent considerable time on their studies. They both knew that their future plans would be highly dependent upon making good grades during this year at Shepherd.

And that dedication to their studies was paying off. They were each making A's in all of their courses. Jenny and her advisor were preparing all of the necessary paperwork that would be required by WVU to apply for the master's degree program in Journalism. This included giving each professor, of the courses she was currently taking, a form to fill out indicating her progress and likely grade for the semester.

Jenny planned to submit her application package the first week after returning to class from the Thanksgiving holiday. If she got accepted into the WVU master's degree program, and everyone was confident that she would, she would hopefully hear by the end of

January. It would be an acceptance with one minor contingency. She would have to send WVU her final transcript with grades for the spring semester and her final grade point average.

Lee, on the other hand, would not be allowed to apply for early entry to WVU's dental school until later in the spring semester at Shepherd. Lee was able to work with his advisor and pre-register for the spring semester in early November. His advisor then alerted all of Lee's upcoming spring course professors about the early entry dental school program. They all agreed to provide a final grade report at the earliest possible time in the spring, hopefully even before the semester was finished, so that the application package could be sent to WVU. Still, it was not likely that Lee would get a final acceptance notification before early June.

Lee and Jenny were doing everything they could to help make their plans become a reality. And they were certainly thankful for the support and encouragement from their advisors and professors at Shepherd.

*   *   *   *   *   *   *

Thanksgiving was rapidly approaching. Lee and Jenny were definitely excited, but a little bit nervous about meeting the parents, too.

"Nothing to worry about, Jenny," Lee assured her, a few days before the Thanksgiving break. "They're going to love you as much as I do."

And yes, the couple had recently told each other that they loved one another. Jenny had cried and Lee was as happy as could be.

"Why are you crying?" Lee asked Jenny. "I thought you would be happy."

"I am happy, silly. These are happy tears, can't you tell?" Jenny asked.

"Well, to be honest, I didn't know there was a difference," Lee admitted.

"Oh, there is," said Jenny. "There definitely is."

I guess I have a lot to learn about girls and emotions and all kinds of things that I never knew about before, Lee thought to himself, as he hugged Jenny.

But back to the upcoming Thanksgiving visit. Jenny wondered what to wear; whether or not to hold Lee's hand; how to act with Rita and Dusty; and even what to call his parents. Should she hug Lee in front of everyone? And even what they were going to eat and drink and her make-up? And then there were things like what shoes to wear. Oh, my! This is going to be so nerve-wracking, she thought.

99

When Jenny asked Lee all of these questions, he just shook his head and told her, "Jenny, just be yourself and play it all by ear. It will all be fine. Just act like you do when we go to a movie or out for dinner. Believe me, my parents are going to love you."

And with that, Jenny said, "Oh Lee, I love you," as she began to cry again and reach out to Lee for a hug.

Lee hugged Jenny and held her tightly. This crying thing is going to take some getting used to, he thought to himself, but I guess these are those happy tears she talks about. At least I hope so.

On Thanksgiving morning, Jenny drove over to the parking lot at the Antietam National Battlefield. She left her car there and Lee picked her up. Knowing how nervous she was, he wanted to be with her as they arrived at the Maxey home.

By 11:00 a.m. Lee pulled into the driveway at the Maxey house. He came around to open the door for her and whispered, "Be calm; this will all be fine. I'll stay right beside you until you feel comfortable with everything."

Ann Maxey had told Lee that they wouldn't eat until about 12:30 or so. That would give them plenty of time to make introductions and visit. And then, if Jenny wanted to, she could help her and Rita with a few things in the kitchen.

"Welcome to the Maxey home," Ann said to Jenny as she met them at the front door with her husband Will. "We're so happy that you were able to come visit us for Thanksgiving, Jenny."

"We sure are," Will added. "Come on in and close that door, Lee; it's cold outside."

Will and Ann each gave Jenny a little hug, took her coat, and led them to the living room, where she was introduced to Rita and Dusty.

"So glad to meet you, Jenny," said Rita, who gave her a hug. "We've heard so much about you from Lee. And this is my husband, Dusty."

"Nice to meet you," Dusty said, reaching out to shake her hand. Turning to Lee, he said, "Wow, Lee, you sure hit the jackpot with her."

"Oh, Dusty, my word," Rita said, playfully smacking Dusty on his shoulder.

Neither Lee or Jenny took any offense to Dusty's remark and just looked at each other, grinned, and embraced in a hug that seemed to come as naturally as anything between the couple.

"Don't pay any attention to my husband," said Rita. "He's just a jock, and he doesn't know how to act sometimes. But he's gentle and means well."

"Not a problem," said Jenny. "I know he meant it as a compliment."

"I did, I did," agreed Dusty. "It's just that she is......."

"Dusty!" Rita interrupted. "That's enough," she told him, as everyone in the room laughed, even Dusty.

After everyone was seated, Ann and Rita told Jenny about being high school English teachers.

"Go, figure, on that," said Lee. "English is my worst subject."

"Mine, too," Dusty chimed in, as everyone laughed again.

They all seemed to be getting along so well.

"Well, I just work for the city here in Hagerstown," Will explained. "Nothing too exciting about that."

"But Lee also told me that you worked on a Forest Service fire crew for a couple of summers during college," Jenny said. "My parents have been involved with that, too; dad years ago when he began work with the Forest Service in Utah before he got into more of an administrative position with the National Park Service. He's now with their parent department at Interior in Washington, D.C. where he can retire in a few years. My mother has served as a Fire Information Officer for some western forest fires, but she doesn't do that anymore. She works in Public Affairs at Antietam and other nearby Park Service locations."

"That's very interesting; seems like we have some things in common," said Will. "Yes, I enjoyed my two summers with the firefighting crew in Idaho. It was kind of exciting at the time, but with a degree in business management from Pitt, I think I'm more suited to the type of work that I'm now in.

"And, by the way," continued Will, "Lee has told us of your plans to attend WVU in Morgantown. I grew up in Fairchance, Pennsylvania, which is only 20 miles from Morgantown. We used to go down there all of the time to shop, attend football games, and so on. But despite all of that I went to college at the University of Pittsburgh, WVU's bitter rival."

"Lee said you are a coach at Frostburg State," Jenny said to Dusty. "I can't remember, is it rugby or something that you coach?"

"No," Dusty responded. "I coach the lacrosse team. But we do have a club team in rugby that plays against WVU on occasion. I played college lacrosse at Frostburg and was able to stay on as an assistant coach for a few years before the head coaching job opened up."

"I don't know much about lacrosse," Jenny admitted.

"Not a lot of people in this area do," said Dusty, "but it was big over on the eastern shore of Maryland where I grew up. I also teach a couple of courses at Frostburg."

"Not in English, either," added Rita, smiling at Dusty. The whole group got a big kick out of that remark.

"Rita and I have to get a couple of things ready in the kitchen before we eat," said Ann. "Do you want to help us, Jenny? The guys can visit some more and then during the meal you can tell us more about your family and your future plans."

"Sure, I'd love to," said Jenny.

*   *   *   *   *   *   *

After the women had gone to the kitchen, Dusty turned to Lee and said, "Hey Lee, I didn't mean to embarrass you and Jenny with what I said earlier. But she really is a .... well, you know what I mean," he said looking over at Will.

"Not a problem," said Lee. "I think Jenny's a knockout, too."

"Okay, there you go," said Dusty. "And also, Mr. M, just so you know, I think Rita is a total babe, too," he said to Will, who just looked down and shook his head, smiling.

Lee got a big kick out of that remark and started laughing.

"What?" Dusty asked, sensing that maybe he had said too much once again. "Maybe I'd better just not say anything else today."

"Probably a good idea," agreed Will.

And once again, Lee couldn't keep from laughing.

*   *   *   *   *   *   *

By 12:30 they were ready to eat. Will offered a Thanksgiving prayer and they all dug in to a wonderful meal. Jenny explained more about her desire to get a double master's degree at WVU; and also why she didn't want to follow exactly in her mother's footsteps with all of the travel and the heavy workload that she had to handle in her public affairs position.

"I can see what you mean by that," Ann said.

"Seems like she's doing the work of two or three people," said Will.

"She pretty much is," agreed Jenny. "A lot of these government agencies have had cutbacks and downsizing and have not been allowed to fill positions when someone retires or transfers. Mom knew that would be the case when she accepted this job. But she and dad wanted to get back closer to home and this was the option that was available at the time."

"We all hope it works out for you with WVU and that you get your acceptance letter in January," Rita said. "I think with your grades, you're a shoe-in. And Lee, you won't know anything about dental school until summer, right?" she asked.

"Yes, probably not until June or so," Lee said. "But my advisor said that it all looks very positive."

"Well, we all have our fingers crossed for both of you," said Ann. "Now, who wants a piece of pumpkin pie and who wants pecan pie?"

"I'll take one of each," said Dusty, before anyone else could answer. "With whipped cream, too. I know there's some of that here because we brought it."

"Dusty," Rita said, giving her husband a look.

"Oh, I'm sorry," Dusty said. "I should have let everyone else say what they wanted first. But I'll still have one of each, if there's plenty to go around."

Rita just shook her head, while everyone else, except Dusty, laughed and laughed.

"I'm sure we'll have plenty," said Ann.

"I think that when we have kids," said Rita, "I'm going to have to be in charge of teaching them manners."

"Another good idea," agreed Will.

After the meal, they all had more time to talk and get to know each other better. When it was time to leave, Jenny thanked everyone for the wonderful meal and the time spent together. They said their goodbye's and Lee and Jenny headed back toward Antietam.

"You have a very nice family, Lee," said Jenny.

"Thanks," Lee said. "And that Dusty is a hoot, isn't he? He's a handful for Rita, that's for sure. But he's good to her and we all like him."

"I think they're all very nice," Jenny replied.

*   *   *   *   *   *   *

Jenny submitted her paperwork to WVU the following week and both she and Lee spent the next three weeks studying, finishing various reports and projects, and taking finals. Thankfully, their course grades were high enough that they each had to take only one final exam.

The supervisors at the AT Visitor Center and also the Harpers Ferry Visitor Center both contacted Jenny about possibly filling in for some people who were wanting to take vacation days for the three-week period starting before Christmas and through New Year's. Jenny happily agreed. She could use the money.

The two supervisors got together and decided upon a split of Jenny's time. It looked like she would be working 10 or 12 days over that timeframe. Still, she was able to meet Lee at the Moon Dog twice and they also went to one movie in Hagerstown.

Their plan was to spend Christmas Eve and Christmas Day with their own families. Then, the next day Lee would meet Jenny mid-morning at the AT Visitor Center and ride in her car over to her parents' house in Harpers Ferry. Parking would be kind of tight at the Lewis house, which is why they would leave Lee's vehicle in the AT parking lot.

*　　*　　*　　*　　*　　*　　*

Lee was a little bit nervous about meeting Jenny's parents, too, but not quite as bad as Jenny had been at Thanksgiving. On Christmas Day, they talked on the phone.

"Is there anything I need to know or be aware of before my visit?" Lee asked her.

"No, just be yourself, as you told me earlier. And yes, they're going to love you," she smiled. "And I'll stay right with you," she laughed.

"Now I know you're making fun of me," Lee said. "But I promise not to cry; even happy tears."

They both laughed into the phone at that comment.

"Oh, Lee, I love you," Jenny said.

"I love you, too," said Lee.

*   *   *   *   *   *   *

Lee met Jenny at the AT Visitor at 10:00 a.m. on the day after Christmas. "Any last minute instructions?" Lee asked her.

"No, are you nervous?" Jenny asked.

"Nope, let's do it," he said. "I'm ready to meet, eat, and shoot some pool."

It was just a short drive to the Lewis home and Paula and Matt met them at the front door. "Come on in, you two," said Paula. "So, this is Lee. Very glad to meet you. Jenny has told us so much about you."

"Glad to meet you, too," said Lee. "I feel like I know you. Jenny has told me so much about your work with the Park Service."

"Hi, Lee," said Matt. "Jenny says you like to shoot pool."

"I do, but she's way better than me," Lee said.

109

"Dad, we haven't even taken our coats off yet and you're already talking about playing pool," said Jenny.

"What's new," said Paula. "That's what he talks about most of the time."

"You're exaggerating, honey. It's not that bad, is it?" Matt asked.

"It's not much of an exaggeration," she smiled.

Once their coats were off and they moved further inside, Lee was introduced to Dave and Nora Smith, Jenny's aunt and uncle; and to her sister, Laura. After talking for a few minutes, Jenny's dad, as expected, suggested they go shoot some pool.

"We won't eat for another hour," said Paula, "so go ahead. We can all visit some more during and after the meal."

So Matt, Jenny, Lee, and Dave went downstairs to shoot some pool, while Nora and Laura helped Paula in the kitchen.

They decided to play 8-ball with Jenny and Lee against Matt and Dave.

"I'm not that good," said Lee. "You'll probably beat us to death."

"Relax, Lee, it's only for fun," said Matt.

Jenny whispered to Lee, "With dad, it's anything but fun. He always tries to win. But like he said, relax. I'm better than my uncle and you probably are, too. We'll do okay."

Matt broke the rack and proceeded to make six balls before he got into a bad position and missed a shot. Jenny went next and she made four balls. Dave missed his shot and then Lee made two before missing. That left Matt to make his team's last ball and then the eight ball to win the game.

"Well, that was closer than I expected," said Matt. "You're not a bad shot, Lee."

"I think we should have won," said Jenny, smiling at her dad.

"That's my girl, but I don't think that's going to happen," said a confident Matt.

"Wait and see," replied Jenny.

Matt told Jenny to break this time and darn if she didn't make two balls; and three more before Dave sunk one. Then it was Lee's turn. He pocketed one ball, before Jenny instructed him on how to play a "safety" shot, completely bottling up Matt, who scratched on his turn. Jenny then made two nice shots to win the game, sinking the eight ball on a nice bank shot. After which she gave Lee a hug.

"Told you so," Jenny said, looking at her dad.

"You taught her too well, Matt," Jenny's uncle said.

"One game apiece," said Matt. "This one's for the championship before we go eat."

Matt got ready to shoot since they were alternating teams for the break.

"Wait a minute," Jenny said. "You already broke once. I have to keep an eye on you. It's Dave's turn."

Dave broke the rack and made no balls. Lee proceeded to make two before Matt stepped up and sank five balls. Jenny made three shots before missing and leaving the table to Dave.

Dave took careful aim and missed his shot; but his cue ball glanced away and accidentally knocked the eight ball in the side pocket to lose the game. Jenny and Lee had won!

"So, I guess we're the champions," said Jenny to her dad.

"Humph," Matt grunted. "Let's go eat."

Once they were upstairs, Paula asked, "Well, who won?"

"Who else?" replied Jenny. "Lee and I won. We're the champs; best two out of three. Right, dad?"

"Humph," Matt grunted.

The meal included ham, scalloped potatoes, green bean casserole, pickled beets, kale, baby carrots, and rolls. What a layout, thought Lee!

"Now, don't stuff yourselves because you have to save room for dessert," said Paula. "We have lemon meringue pie or brownies with vanilla ice cream; or both if you'd like. We have plenty."

"Dusty would love that," Lee whispered to Jenny, as they smiled at one another.

"And for drinks we have iced tea, water, coffee, or diet cola," added Paula.

Jenny's uncle Dave said grace and everyone was ready to eat.

During the meal, Lee explained his plans for dental school and told the Lewis' about his parents' professions. He mentioned that his dad had worked for the Forest Service in Idaho as a firefighter for two summers before going to work for the City of Hagerstown.

"I helped fight a few fires in my early years in Utah and Arizona with the Forest Service," Matt said.

"But after I transferred over to the Park Service, my main role with forest fires was in the accounting, payroll, and purchasing areas."

"And my role with forest fires," added Paula, "has always been in Fire Information – sometimes assigned directly to a large fire on the ground at a fire camp; and at other times in more of an area-wide or regional support role," she explained. "More often than not, I end up writing and sending out news releases; accompanying reporters to see something on the ground; or fielding various media inquiries on the phone."

"Well, I find it all very interesting and important," said Lee. "I'm sure you do, too."

"It sounds like you and Jenny will both be at WVU next year," commented Nora.

"That will be great, if it works out," said Lee.

"And we have our fingers crossed on that," added Jenny.

For dessert, Lee had the brownie and vanilla ice cream, while Jenny had a piece of lemon meringue pie, her favorite.

"What a great meal, Mrs. Lewis. Thank you very much," Lee said.

"How about a piece of pie?" she asked.

"No, thank you," said Lee. "I'm stuffed."

After the meal, Matt, Dave, and Nora helped Paula with the clean-up, while Jenny and Lee had a chance to visit with Laura, who was very nice and seemed to be quite a dedicated nurse. She was an RN and worked as the lead office nurse for an obstetrics-gynecology group in South Charleston.

"Jenny said you went to WVU for two years, before transferring to Marshall to finish your training," said Lee.

"Yes," replied Laura. "You probably wonder why I did that, but I had some personal things going on and I needed a change of scenery. I had a couple of good friends at Marshall, so that made the transfer go much easier than it could have been. I'm happy with the way things worked out."

She didn't seem to want to talk more about that, so Lee let it drop. Jenny told Laura that hopefully once she and Lee got settled in with their studies at Morgantown, they would try their best to come down to Charleston for a visit. Laura thought that would be great.

Dave and Nora had to leave soon after everyone was finished eating. They had some things to do back at their farm.

Matt asked Lee if he'd like to shoot some more pool and Lee eagerly agreed. Unfortunately for Lee, they played four games of eight-ball and Matt won them all. But it was great fun, for sure.

While the two men played pool, Jenny and Laura had a chance to talk with their mother about a variety of things.

Soon, Lee was saying his goodbye's and thanking everyone for a great visit. They had all seemed to get along very well.

Later, as Jenny took Lee back to his car at the AT parking lot, she explained things further in regard to Laura's transfer from WVU to Marshall.

"When Laura was in junior high school she began dating a boy in her class," said Jenny. "His name was Paul. They had known each other for a few years, but began dating after attending a summer church camp over in Morgan County. In the 10th grade his family moved to Martinsburg, but they continued to date. They went to school dances at each other's schools and saw each other as often as possible. He became a star football player at Martinsburg High School and got a scholarship to WVU," Jenny explained.

"Well, they were both attending WVU and they had gotten engaged when they were sophomores over there," continued Jenny. "Just before the end of their sophomore year, Paul had to come back to Martinsburg for a family event one weekend. Laura was deep into studying for finals, so she had stayed in Morgantown. Thank goodness for that. On his way back to Morgantown a tractor trailer sideswiped a car on the other side of Interstate 68. The driver lost control and swerved across the median, hitting Paul's car head on and killing him instantly."

"That's terrible," said Lee. "What a tragedy."

"For sure," said Jenny. "It was a shock to everyone. Laura was so devastated. We were sad about Paul. We all liked him so much. Laura had a tough time accepting it all. I don't know how she finished the semester, but she did. Soon after that, she told mom and dad that she couldn't go back to WVU," Jenny explained. "A friend of Laura's was attending Marshall and she decided to transfer down there. She still wanted to be a nurse, but just couldn't cope with returning to Morgantown."

"Wow," Lee said. "No wonder she doesn't want to talk about it. I can't imagine going through something like that."

"We're still not sure she's completely over it," Jenny went on, "but she graduated with honors at Marshall, got a good job that she loves in South Charleston, and has actually begun to date a little bit over the past few months. I was a senior in high school when the accident happened."

"I'm so sorry for all of you to have gone through that," said Lee. "I love you, Jenny. And you have a wonderful family."

*   *   *   *   *   *   *

Jenny and Lee went on dates twice more before the spring semester began at Shepherd. They talked on the phone every night. And Jenny went to a New Year's Eve party at the Maxey home. The Maxey's had a spare bedroom, so Jenny spent the night there instead of having to be on the road late that evening.

School started the second week in January and before the end of the month Jenny received confirmation that she was accepted into the graduate program in journalism at WVU. Great news! She would just have to send them a final copy of her spring semester grades and her final grade point average.

The couple was really happy. So far, so good. Now Lee just had to keep his grades up and send in his application for dental school, hopefully in April so that he could hear something by June.

The couple ate more than one meal at the Moon Dog, their favorite spot, during the semester and attended three Shepherd basketball games. But mostly they studied, Lee extremely hard. He did not want to have to spend one more year at Shepherd while Jenny was in Morgantown.

Lee did find the time to enjoy two Sunday meals at the Lewis home and, yes, to shoot a few games of pool with Jenny's dad. Jenny also joined the Maxey's for two Sunday afternoon meals. Both families were expecting this couple to stay together........for a long time. They just seemed to get along so well.

Lee was making A's on every test and every paper; so, his advisor was able to convince all of Lee's professors to submit his final grades by mid-April. The rest of the paperwork was already prepared and waiting to submit, so the entire package was sent to WVU just a couple of days later.

Lo and behold, by the first week in June, Lee received notice that he had been accepted into the early entry program in the WVU dental school.

"I love it when a plan comes together," Lee said happily when he gave the news to Jenny that evening at the Moon Dog. They sat at a corner table in the back and hugged and kissed, and then hugged and kissed some more. And yes, Jenny cried. Happy tears. The third time the waitress came around they figured they had better order something or risk getting thrown out.

"Now we just have to make sure we find a place to live in Morgantown," said Lee after they placed their order. "Should we try to find a place together?" he asked Jenny.

"That would be great, as far as I'm concerned, but maybe we'd better wait on that," she replied. "It might not be the right thing to do and I'm sure our parents wouldn't approve."

"I guess you're right," Lee agreed. "But what do you say, if we see how things progress the first year at WVU, and then if we get engaged, like we've already talked about, maybe we could do that the next year. You'd be in your final year of grad school by then," he said.

"Sounds reasonable to me," Jenny said, as she leaned over for more hugging and kissing.

Looking up, they noticed the waitress waiting impatiently with their food.

"Sorry," Lee said to the waitress.

"That's okay," she laughed. "I was enjoying watching the two of you lovebirds."

Jenny soon found lodging for herself in one of the University Apartments. Her WVU journalism advisor was able to pair her up with another incoming journalism female grad student from West Liberty University, who was looking for a roommate. The advisor had been able to put a hold on a two-bedroom, two-bath apartment just a short walk from the journalism school on the downtown campus. They had to make a final decision within a few days. Jenny called the other girl, who lived in Wheeling; they talked, and seemed to have similar goals and interests, so they decided to lock it in. Arrangements were made and now it was up to Lee to take care of his lodging.

The WVU dental program kept a list of incoming students who would be needing lodging or who were looking for roommates. On the list was a first-year student from Keyser named Monty Barnes. Lee called and talked with him.

Monty had attended Potomac State College in Keyser before transferring to WVU to complete his BS degree in Biology. He had roomed with a friend while doing this. That friend had graduated and was moving to take a job in Ohio. Once Monty was accepted into the dental program at WVU, he decided it would be best if he could find a roommate who was also a dental school student. That all made sense to Lee.

Lee explained his situation to Monty and told him that after a year at WVU he planned to get engaged and might be moving in with his fiancée that following year. Monty was okay with that because he said at their age, things always seemed to change from year to year anyway. At least this would solve the housing problem for the first year.

The two students had a lot in common, too. Monty had a friend who had attended Shepherd University, which was only a couple of hours from Keyser. The more they talked the more they seemed to get along, so they decided to go with this arrangement for the upcoming year. Monty had already put down a deposit on a two-person apartment within walking distance to the WVU Health Sciences Center, which housed the dental program. In the following days Lee and Monty finalized all of their lodging arrangements for the coming year.

*   *   *   *   *   *   *

For the rest of the summer, Lee and Jenny talked on the phone every day. They met as often as possible for lunch, dinner, or at their parents' homes for visits. Jenny was able to work a full-time schedule at the Harpers Ferry Visitor Center until time to leave for Morgantown. The money she saved would come in handy at WVU.

Lee continued to work two or three evenings a week at the bakery and he picked up a few odd jobs in Hagerstown through contacts that his dad had in town. He also earned a little extra cash by helping one of his Shepherd professors move into a new house in Shepherdstown. The money that Lee saved would also be very helpful when he moved to Morgantown.

So, things were working out as planned. Lee and Jenny were so happy when they were together, they almost seemed like a married couple.

"Did those two get married and I missed the wedding?" Matt Lewis playfully asked his wife, Paula.

"No, at least I don't think so," replied Paula with a laugh. "But I can't believe how loving they are toward each other. I think this is going to be a long-term husband and wife pairing. Jenny told me that they will probably get engaged within a year."

"Is that so?" said Matt. "I'm always the last to know. I hope I get invited to the wedding," he laughed.

"Well then, you'd better let Lee beat you once in a while when you play pool," she said.

"Not going to happen," said Matt. "I'm not going to 'let' him win anything. He'll have to beat me fair and square. But to be honest with you, he's getting closer and closer to that happening."

Will and Ann Maxey were equally pleased with their son and Jenny.

"I really like Jenny," Ann said to Will one evening. "She's so smart and has a really strong desire to succeed in journalism."

"I like her, too," said Will. "The two of them seem to get along so well, it's almost like they're already married."

"From what Rita told me last week, that may not be too far in the future," said Ann. "I guess Lee and Jenny are already talking about a formal engagement in the near future."

"I've been expecting that," Will replied. "I just hope they can both continue doing well with their school work."

"I don't have any doubts about that," Ann said. "Lee really wants to be a dentist and Jenny seems so driven that I don't think either of them will slack off on their academic commitments."

"I think you're right," Will agreed.

The future was indeed bright for Lee and Jenny. It had been extremely fortunate that they had met in Harpers Ferry nearly a year ago. Though it had certainly been a series of things that led to them becoming a committed couple, they always told friends that their love began during a Harpers Ferry holiday.

Chapter 4

WE MET AT LAIDLEY FIELD

J. P. Galford had checked into his motel in Charleston on Friday and headed over to Laidley Field to watch some of the state track meet that afternoon. The Class AA events would be taking place and then later that evening he would watch his sister, Hannah, run in the Class AAA 3200 meter race for Greenbrier East High School.

J.P. liked track, although he was now a freshman playing baseball for Concord University in Athens, West Virginia. His baseball team would be coming to the University of Charleston early tomorrow morning for a double header against the Golden Eagles. The first of the two seven-inning games would start at 1:00 p.m., so his team would not leave Athens for the 1 ½ hour drive to Charleston until early Saturday morning. They would stay overnight and play another double header on Sunday afternoon. J.P.'s coach had given him permission to travel to Charleston a day early, so that he could watch his sister run in the state track meet.

Hannah was not one of the favorites in the 3200 meter race, but she was just a junior and she had become more and more competitive as the year went on. She had high hopes for both the 3200 and the 1600 meter races for her senior year. Heck, J.P. thought to himself, it was an honor just to qualify to run in the state meet and he wanted to be there to support his sister.

J.P. had been a standout on the baseball team at Greenbrier East and when Concord offered him a scholarship, he jumped at the chance. He now started in left field most games for the Mountain Lions and had a batting average that hovered around the .300 mark for the year. He had good speed and was leading the team in stolen bases and walks.

J.P. had dabbled in track in middle school and as a high school sophomore. He loved running track and he loved all of the activities surrounding the meets. He had recorded some pretty decent times in both the 110 high hurdles and the 300 intermediate hurdles early his sophomore year. But with the scheduling conflicts between baseball and track, he eventually gave up his career as a track hurdler to concentrate on baseball. Still, he loved to watch a good track meet, especially one where his sister and other friends were competing.

Once J.P. got to Laidley Field, he grabbed some food and settled in to watch the rest of the events of the AA portion of the state meet. The first event he watched was the girls 1600 meter finals. It was quite an even race for the first three laps, but on the final lap a girl from Winfield pulled away for a comfortable win over a girl from PikeView.

PikeView High School was located only a few miles from Concord and J.P. was happy to see a runner from his area do well.

After the 1600 meter boys race, J.P. got to watch hurdles, sprints, sprint relays, and finally, just after 5:00 p.m., the AA portion of the meet concluded with both the girls and boys 4 x 400 meter relays.

He thought to himself again that he really enjoyed watching a good track meet. During the afternoon he had a chance to talk with a few former classmates from Greenbrier East and also with his sister, to wish her good luck in her upcoming race. Hannah really appreciated her brother coming to Charleston a day early to watch her run.

After a break of an hour or so, following the AA awards ceremony, his sister was scheduled to run in the finals of the AAA 3200 meter race. He would miss the rest of the AAA meet on Saturday because of his baseball game, but that was okay. He was there primarily to see his sister run anyway.

J.P. went down to the concession stand to get something to eat before watching his sister run. While standing in line, he noticed in front of him was the girl from PikeView High School who had finished second in the 1600 meter race.

She happened to turn around and J.P. said, "Hey, congratulations on that silver medal you won earlier."

"Thanks, but I just couldn't keep up with the girl from Winfield on that last lap," she replied. "She's really good. I hear that she has been offered a scholarship to run at the University of Kentucky. I ran a 5:30 time, which is pretty good though."

"It sure is," said J.P. "My sister runs the 1600 and she has never run that fast. She did qualify for states in the 3200 meter run though, which is starting in an hour or so. She runs for Greenbrier East and I came to watch her. She's just a junior, so we have high hopes for her senior year."

"So, do you go to Greenbrier East, too?" she asked. "I notice that you have a Concord University T-shirt on. That college is not far from my high school, PikeView."

"I went to Greenbrier East, but I'm now a student at Concord," J.P. explained. "And I know where PikeView is. I was kind of cheering for you when you ran because it is so close to Concord."

"Oh, wow, thanks. What's your name anyway?" she asked.

"I'm J.P. Galford; and you are......? he asked.

"I'm Emily Adams. Nice to meet you, J.P.," she said.

This girl is really pretty, J.P. thought to himself as he watched her order her food. He then stepped up to the window to place his order.

That's a really nice guy, Emily thought to herself, and so cute, too.

J.P. got his food and turned to go. He was surprised, but pleased, that Emily had waited for him.

"I thought you were gone," he said. "But I'm glad that you're still here. Want to sit up in the stands and watch my sister run her race?"

"Sure, that would be great," Emily replied. "But then after the race, I'll have to go back over to where our team is sitting. We'll board the bus soon after that for the ride back home."

J.P. and Emily had about 45 minutes before Hannah was to run, so there was some time to visit. Also, there were two AAA finals in the girls and boys 400 meter races that they got to watch.

"So, I guess you don't run track at Concord then?" Emily asked.

"Oh, no," said J.P. "I'm a freshman on the baseball team there. We play a doubleheader tomorrow against the University of Charleston. Coach let me come up a day early so that I could see my sister run. The rest of the team is coming up early tomorrow morning. Our games start at 1:00 p.m."

"My dad has gone over to Concord to watch some baseball games," Emily said. "He's a big baseball fan. He has probably seen you play. I'll have to come over with him and watch a game."

"That would be great," said J.P. "Let me know when you're going to be there. I'll give you my cell phone number. Can I get your number, too?"

"Sure," replied Emily. "And by the way, Concord is one of two schools that are recruiting me to run track. The other one is the University of Pikeville over in Kentucky. It's an NAIA school, whereas Concord is NCAA Division II. People say there is not much difference in the competition level between those two affiliations. But I don't really know."

"That's what I've always heard, too," said J.P. "Just about all of the schools in our conference used to be NAIA before they switched to NCAA Division II. Our coach told me when I was recruited that the DII schools spend a little more money on their overall athletic programs and they generally offer more full scholarships than NAIA schools. But again, I'm not 100 percent sure about that. Either way, I think that playing sports in college is great. And if you can get some scholarship assistance to help out with your education, that is great, too."

"Pikeville wants me to run both track and cross country, but the Concord coach said that I could do track only," said Emily, "but maybe run in two or three separate events. They run a 1500 or 1600 meter race in some meets and then something like a 5000 meter run, also. That's a little long for me; I guess it takes some getting used to for that length of race. The coach said he might even try me in the 3000 meter steeplechase. I've never run that race, but it sounds interesting.

"I'm not really interested in running cross country like Pikeville wants, either," continued Emily. "I guess I would do it if it meant not having to pay as much out of pocket for my education. Since Concord is just a few miles from where I live, the coach told me that if I would live at home the first year, they would cover all of my other costs – tuition, books, fees, meals, and everything else. Then, if things work out, the second year, after some of the seniors graduate, he could put me on a full scholarship, including paying for my room on campus, too."

"That sounds good," said J.P. "I'm on a half scholarship, but coach has promised to try and increase that for future years. We have a few guys on a full ride, but most of us are on partial scholarships."

"So, did you run the 3200 meter race last night, as well as the 1600 today?" J.P. asked.

"Yes," responded Emily. "I finished third in the 3200. The same girl from Winfield won that race, too. She's amazing. I ran about a 12:15, which was good for me, but I was nosed out for second by a girl from Berkeley Springs. She told me she is considering college offers from Davis & Elkins, as well as Frostburg State over in Maryland, which she said is only an hour from where she lives.

"The Concord coach has watched me run a few times this year and he thinks he can really help me improve my times quite a bit if I go to school there. I'm leaning toward Concord over Pikeville."

"I think that would be great," said J.P., looking over at Emily and smiling. "By the way, are your parents here?"

"Yes, they're on the other side of the field. I talked with them after my race, but I'm going to ride home with the team on the bus," said Emily.

Soon it was time for J.P.'s sister Hannah to run in the 3200 meter race. She ran a good race, but finished in the middle of the pack. A girl from Morgantown High School won the race.

Emily had to go join her teammates before the boys 3200 race began, while J.P. wanted to go down and congratulate his sister on a good race. They exchanged phone numbers and said their goodbye's. J.P. promised to call Emily in a few days.

I'm sure glad I met her, J.P. thought to himself. She's so pretty and easy to talk with. She's quite an athlete, too. I hope she decides to go to Concord.

Emily joined her teammates in the stands, where they had begun to take down their sun tent and pack up. "Where have you been," a couple of her friends, Jenny and Susan, asked her, "flirting with boys from other schools?"

"No, not really," Emily told them. "But I did meet a cute guy who plays baseball for Concord. They are up here to play against the University of Charleston tomorrow. His sister just ran in the AAA 3200 meter race and we watched that together."

"Just like we figured," her teammates kidded her. "Always flirting with the boys; only this time it's a college guy. I guess you're moving on from high school boys."

"Well, J.P. is just a freshman at Concord, so he can't be that much older than I am," Emily replied, as her face turned red.

"J.P.?" they both asked at the same time. "So, you know his name. Don't tell me you gave him your phone number, too."

"Well, maybe I did," said Emily, "but I got his phone number, also."

Susan and Jenny both began laughing, and then all three girls hugged and continued laughing together. They were best friends and had known each other for several years.

*   *   *   *   *   *   *

J.P. stopped at a restaurant on the way back to his motel and ate a good dinner with meal money that the coach had given him. His parents, Linda and Bob Galford, had not been able to attend the track meet today because his mom's father had been admitted to a hospital near where he lived in Covington, Virginia.

J.P.'s grandfather, Woody Johnson, lived by himself in Covington and getting accurate information about what the problem was had been difficult. A neighbor had taken him to the hospital on Thursday evening and then called J.P.'s mother. His grandfather had evidently developed considerable pain in his stomach or side, or maybe both.

The hospital was less than an hour from where the Galford's lived outside of Lewisburg and they had decided to drive over that evening. They wanted to attend the state track meet to watch Hannah run, but thought they should go over to Covington instead.

Once they arrived at the hospital, they found that Mr. Johnson had had to have an emergency appendectomy. In fact, he had let the pain go for a day or so and the appendix was ready to burst. In addition, it had begun to leak, which was a problem. Once the doctors had begun work on removing the appendix and doing some cleanup where it had leaked, they had also discovered a rather large hernia in the stomach area. That needed to be corrected, too; so with the two medical procedures, the surgeon decided to keep Woody in the hospital until Saturday morning. And when he got home someone would need to stay with him for a few days until his recovery was well along.

J.P.'s parents had called him a couple of times to keep him posted on his grandfather's condition. They had also called Hannah and explained what was going on, but not to worry because her grandfather was doing just fine.

The Galford's had stayed in the Johnson house in Covington on Thursday night and were able to spend Friday at the hospital, talking with the doctor and other medical staff, as well as being there to comfort Woody. Linda decided to stay in Covington to help her dad for a few days, while Bob returned to Lewisburg Friday night. Linda was an elementary school teacher in Lewisburg and could take a few personal leave days as needed. Her principal was very understanding in these type of situations.

Linda always kept spare clothes and toiletries at her dad's house because there had been numerous times when she had had to stay over there to help out with things since her mother's death a few years ago. And she would have her dad's car to use as needed.

Linda had been trying to talk her dad into moving to Lewisburg near them, but he had lived in the Covington area all of his life and didn't want to leave. He had retired from the MeadWestvaco paper mill, where he worked for over 35 years. Most of the friends he had grown up with and worked with at the mill still lived in the area. They usually met for coffee two or three mornings a week. Woody always said that he wanted to live in Covington until he died.

Linda called Bob from the hospital on Saturday morning early and told him that her dad was feeling much better. But as usual, they weren't sure when he would be released; hopefully around noon or so.

After getting the good report from Linda, Bob decided to drive to Charleston to watch J.P.'s baseball games. If he left home by 9:00 a.m., he could be there in plenty of time to grab a quick bite to eat and pick up

Hannah before the game started at one o'clock. She was not running any track events that day, but was still there to support her teammates. But she would go with her dad to J.P.'s Saturday games before they returned home Saturday evening. Bob would miss J.P.'s Sunday doubleheader, but he and Hannah would attend church in Lewisburg before driving over to Covington to check on Linda and her dad.

*   *   *   *   *   *   *

Bob arrived at the Laidley Field parking lot where he had told Hannah to meet him at 10:30 a.m. They went to a Charleston deli for an early lunch and were at the baseball field shortly after noon, so they could watch the teams warm up and take batting practice.

Since Concord was the visiting team, they were using the dugout on the third base side of the field. As Bob and Hannah made their way to their seats, they saw J.P. and he was talking to a girl who was standing at the railing near the dugout. As they got closer, Hannah waved and yelled out, "Hey, J.P."

J.P. saw his dad and sister and waved back. "Hey sis; hey dad. Glad you made it."

Walking down the steps toward the dugout, Hannah recognized the girl as one who had run in the AA track meet the previous evening.

137

"Hi," Hannah said, "I think I saw you run the 1600 meter race last evening, didn't I?"

"Yes, and J.P. and I watched you run the AAA 3200 meter race not long after that, too," said Emily.

"I can't remember what school you ran for," said Hannah.

"It was PikeView, and my name is Emily Adams. I just met your brother yesterday. We live near Athens, where Concord University is located and my dad goes over to watch some of their baseball games. He's a big baseball fan," Emily said. "When I told him that Concord was playing two games at the University of Charleston today, he decided to come up and watch the games. It only takes about an hour and a half to drive up here."

"Did you stay here last night?" Hannah asked.

"No, I went back on the team bus last night, but after I told dad that I had met J.P., he said he was definitely going to come and watch the games today," said Emily. "He has seen J.P. play at Concord and said he is a really good player. I decided to come along with dad. His name is Al and he's sitting up there in the stands."

"Emily, this is my dad, Bob, who's here today with my sis," J.P. said. "I'll let you all talk, but I have to get back over to the batting cage and take a few swings.

I doubt that I will be able to visit much between games, but hopefully we'll have some time together after the second game. And thank all of you for coming today."

Hannah and her dad walked with Emily up to where Mr. Adams was sitting, introduced themselves, and had some time to talk before the game started.

"That son of yours is a good ballplayer," Al Adams remarked to Bob Galford. "We live out in the country down in Mercer County about halfway between Princeton and Athens. I've been over to Concord to watch a few games this season. J.P.'s a good leadoff hitter.

"He seems to draw a lot of walks and beats out infield groundballs, too," continued Mr. Adams. "One game I saw at Concord earlier this season against Fairmont State, J.P. got a leadoff walk, stole second base, and then third base, too. He scored on a sacrifice fly right after that. Concord beat Fairmont twice in a doubleheader that day."

"I remember that," said Bob Galford. "I was at that game, too."

"You should have come over and said hello," said Al Adams. "Of course, we didn't know each other then," he said with a grin, as the two men shared a laugh.

Emily told Hannah about her possibly getting a track scholarship to run at Concord next year. Hannah was really impressed with that and said that would be her goal, too; but she wasn't sure her times would be good enough to run in college.

"You looked pretty good when J.P. and I watched you in the 3200 meter race yesterday," Emily said. "You were right up there with the leaders for over half the race. They just pulled away on the last lap and a half. You're just a junior, so I think you'll get stronger by next year and do really well. Maybe we can work out and train together some, if we can figure out a way to make that happen."

"That would be awesome," said Hannah. "Running and working out with a college athlete would help me improve my times, I'm sure."

"It would help me, too," replied Emily. "Let's just plan on it if things work out."

Soon, the baseball game started and everyone settled in to watch Concord face Charleston. The first game turned out to be a pitcher's duel and Charleston won the seven-inning contest by a score of 2-1. J.P. drew a walk, struck out once, and got a bloop single to right field, but was wiped out on a nice double play by the Golden Eagles infield. J.P. caught two routine fly balls in left field and made a nice running catch on a sinking line drive off the bat of Charleston's clean-up hitter.

The second game couldn't have been any more different from the first game, as Concord scored early and often, beating Charleston by a score of 10 – 5. J.P. drew two walks and had a double and single in five at-bats. He stole two bases, scored three runs, and had an RBI on the double down the right field line.

Both families enjoyed the doubleheader and had a chance to talk more as they waited for J.P. after the games.

"Great games," Al remarked to Bob. "And your son was a big reason they won that second game. I really like watching him play."

"Well, thanks," said Bob. "I think he's doing really well for a freshman and he loves the game, that's for sure."

"You can tell that from watching him," said Al. "He's kind of the sparkplug for Concord, it seems."

"J.P.'s coach told him recently that he can get him a roster spot to play on Bluefield's summer team in the collegiate league," Bob commented. "And he's excited about that opportunity. It's only about a half hour to Bluefield from Concord, so it would work out well in that regard. His Concord coach has a garage apartment out back from where he lives in Athens and he said J.P. could use that for the summer. I guess some of the players on the team will come from other areas of the country and will be housed with local families in the Bluefield area. As I understand it, the league is for college freshmen and sophomores. They mostly play against teams in Virginia and Tennessee, and I think J.P. said there is one team in the league that is located in North Carolina. They travel to games by bus.

"And, I almost forgot," Bob continued, "there is also a team from Princeton in the league. That would have been great if J.P. could play on that team, but his coach had contacts with the Bluefield officials and not those at Princeton. I guess it's not that big of a deal, since Bluefield is pretty close to Athens, too."

"That sounds interesting," commented Al. "From what I've seen of J.P., I'm sure he could do well against players from other colleges. I'll have to go down to Bluefield to watch a couple of games. Or maybe I can see them when they come to Princeton to play."

Emily had been eavesdropping on the conversation the two fathers were having and couldn't help herself by chiming in to say that "J.P. could always stay with us for the summer, dad."

Al and Bob looked at each other, smiled, and said almost simultaneously, "I don't think so."

"Well, I was just trying to be helpful," Emily said, with a grin on her face.

"Nice try, girl," Hannah said, leaning over to whisper in Emily's ear. "I'm sure J.P. would like that, too."

J.P. had showered, changed clothes, and soon joined the group. "Thank all of you for coming," he told them. "I wish we could have won both games, but a split with Charleston is not bad. They are a good team. There are two or three guys on their team that I played against in high school."

"You played well, son," remarked Bob.

"You sure did," said Al.

"I think you were the best player out there," said Emily, as she rushed over to give J.P. a big hug.

J.P. returned the hug, as the two fathers just looked at each other.

"How long have you two known each other, anyway?" asked Bob.

"I know the answer to that," said Hannah. "It's been about 24 hours. Right guys?"

"More or less," said J.P., "but it already seems longer than that to me."

"Me, too," Emily said, smiling at him.

"Well, let's all go and get something to eat before we head back home," Al said.

"Will that be okay with your coach?" Bob asked J.P.

"He's fine with it," said J.P. "I told him that I would probably do that and he said it would be okay. You'll just have to drop me off at the motel where our team is staying after we finish eating."

"I know a nice restaurant not far from here," Al told the group. "What say you all follow me there?" he said to Bob. "My treat."

"Do you mind if J.P. rides with us, dad?" Emily asked.

"No, of course not, if everyone else is okay with it," Al replied, glancing around and noticing that J.P. and Emily had already begun walking together toward the parking lot.

"Looks like J.P. wants to ride with us," Al said to Bob.

"I see that," said Bob. "I think those two plan on getting to know each other better, don't you?"

"Sure seems like it," muttered Al. "Anyway, just follow me to the restaurant."

*   *   *   *   *   *   *

The group of five soon arrived at the restaurant and were seated at a corner table with plenty of room for them all to spread out. Everyone that is, except for J.P. and Emily, who sat very close to one another. The waitress took the orders and conversations began so that they could all get to know one another better.

"So, what line of work are you in down in Mercer County?" Bob asked Al Adams.

"I'm a consulting forester, working with several individual private landowners, as well as three or four companies who own large tracts of forest land in the southern counties," Al replied.

"Interesting," said Bob. "A good friend I went to high school with is a forester, too. He used to work for the Jefferson National Forest down around Wise, Virginia. He got his forestry degree from West Virginia University and then a master's degree from Virginia Tech. I don't know if you've ever run into him or not, but his name is Rodney Lathems."

"Sure have," answered Al. "I often do work for companies who own large tracts of forest land – coal companies, railroads, timber companies, and so forth. One company had me supervise a logging job on their land down in that area a few years ago, kind of between Wise and Norton, Virginia. We had to obtain a road right-of-way from the U.S. Forest Service to access part of the job and I handled that for the company. I dealt with Rodney to get that permit. Nice guy. He was the District Ranger in that area, as I recall."

"I think that's right," said Bob, "but yes, that would have been a few years ago. Last time I talked with him, he had taken a promotion to the headquarters office in Roanoke. I don't see him very often, but we have our 30th high school reunion coming up next year and he'll probably come to that. I'll ask him if he remembers you."

"I went to forestry school at WVU, too," said Al. "But I would have been a few years ahead of Rodney, I guess. And besides that, I ended up transferring to the University of Kentucky for my final two years. My dad was a highway engineer and he took a job with the state of Kentucky in their Lexington office. It just made sense for me to transfer to UK. One of the professors there had received his bachelor's and master's degrees from WVU. He was very helpful in getting me transferred in to UK and set up as an incoming junior in their forestry program.

"Dad had worked for the West Virginia Division of Highways for a number of years," Al continued. "He was assigned to the District Office in Princeton, but a friend of his got him an interview in Kentucky. It was much better pay and he decided to take the job. It had a lot to do with bridge design and reconstruction, which was more or less his specialty. He ended up retiring from that job and now he and my mother live right up against the Daniel Boone National Forest just outside of Somerset, Kentucky. He had worked on a bridge project over Lake Cumberland near Somerset the last couple of years before he retired. He had to stay down there for several days from time to time and mom would often join him. They really liked that area and decided to retire there.

"After I graduated from UK, I took a job as a landowner assistance forester with the state of West Virginia in Beckley," said Al. "I had grown up in Princeton and was still dating my high school sweetheart, Rita. It was less than an hour from Beckley to Princeton, so I drove down there quite a bit. To make a long story short, we got married and had a daughter. That would be Miss Emily here. We lived in Shady Spring, which was about 10 miles from the Division of Forestry office, for five years. After that, based on what I knew about the forestry situation in the southern counties, I left the state job and hung out my shingle as a private consulting forester. We moved back home to Mercer County and things have worked out quite well for us."

"Wow, I didn't even know all of that," said Emily, who had been listening intently.

"Well, there are a lot of things you don't know, young lady, but that's all I'm going to reveal right now," Al said with a laugh. "Let's change the subject. How about you, Bob? What do you do over in Lewisburg?"

Just as Bob was about to answer, the waitress brought the orders and everyone started to dig in. "First, a toast to new friends," said Al.

"Hear, hear; I'll second that," Bob said. "Let's eat and I'll answer Al's question as we do."

Bob Galford said that he was a supervisor in the Office of Business Affairs for the West Virginia School of Osteopathic Medicine. "We handle the financial affairs of the school, including accounting, payroll, benefits, purchasing, shipping & receiving, accounts payable, and a few other related things. The school is ranked as one of the top medical schools in the nation for training primary care and family medicine doctors," Bob explained. "According to our officials, we are the country's number one medical school for producing doctors who practice in rural areas."

"That's pretty awesome," said Emily.

"I'll say," said Al.

Bob went on to explain that he had received his degree in Finance with a minor in Economics from the Business School at Marshall University in Huntington before getting hired as a trainee at the medical school in Lewisburg. "It was great for me, since I had grown up in that area. I love it and have been there almost 25 years now," Bob said. "My wife Linda is a grade school teacher in Lewisburg. We met at Marshall. She was originally from Spencer and was two years behind me in college. We got married the summer after she graduated from Marshall and we have lived in Lewisburg ever since. And as you know, we have two children – J.P. and Hannah. We thought about having another child, but these two were such a handful that we decided not to," Bob said with a slight grin on his face.

"Da-a-ad," Hannah objected. "What a terrible thing to say."

"Just kidding," said Bob. "They've been model kids. Couldn't have asked for any better."

"Does your wife work?" Bob asked Al.

"Yes, she works about three days a week as an office assistant for a realtor in Princeton," Al said. "It's very flexible and the days vary from week to week, but she likes it that way. She also works an average of one or two days a week helping with insurance billings for a dentist in town. She's friends with the main office manager there and they call her when they start getting backed up with work. It's usually pretty easy for her to work that out around her realty schedule."

"This was a good choice for a restaurant to eat at, Mr. Adams," said Hannah.

"Sure is," agreed J.P. "The food is great and so is the company," he said, smiling at Emily. "Especially the company."

"I agree with that," Emily said with a grin.

"Well, now that Bob and I have given you a mini-version of our lives, you two lovebirds aren't going to get off very easy either," said Al, looking directly at J.P. "I know you play baseball for Concord, but what are your plans for the future, young man."

J.P. noticed that Mr. Adams wasn't necessarily giving him the evil eye or anything like that, but he could tell that he was expecting a serious answer.

"Well," J.P. began, as he nervously cleared his throat, "I have listed my major for the time being as general studies, but I expect to change it to something more specific after the first semester of my sophomore year. My athletic department advisor and I have discussed sports management or possibly accounting, along the lines of what dad does at the osteopathic school. I could see me going in either direction. My next semester will give me a clearer idea of what to pursue my degree in," said J.P.

"That sounds like you have at least begun to think seriously about your future," said Al, "but what exactly would you do with a degree in sports management? Would you coach or something?"

"I guess that's always a possibility, but people with degrees in sports management often end up in the business end of sports," J.P. replied. "They handle the behind the scenes things, such as finance, community relations, marketing, facility management, and special events management. Many athletic directors also have degrees in sports management. So, there are a lot of ways you could go with that degree. Some graduates go to work in professional sports and some in colleges. From what my advisor said, it is often recommended to get a graduate degree in the field. Grad students usually get placed in summer jobs and internships in the field to get experience. He told me that both WVU and Marshall have graduate programs in that field, as well as a highly rated master's degree program at Ohio University in Athens, Ohio."

"Sounds like you're definitely thinking about your future," said Mr. Adams. "I like that."

"Me, too," said Bob Galford. "That's more than you've shared with me son," Bob said, looking over at J.P. "But it all sounds good."

"I like a man with a plan," Emily giggled and looked up at J.P., as she nervously thought to herself, 'why in the world did I just say that?'

"Well, Miss Emily, now that you've spoken up, what kind of future are you thinking of?" Mr. Galford asked.

"Go ahead, Emily, your mother and I have been wondering about that, also," said her dad.

"Give me a break, please," Emily responded. "I haven't even graduated from high school yet. But dad, as you know, both Concord and Pikeville want me to run track for them. And since Concord has such a stellar girls track program and great academics, among other things, I am leaning toward going there."

"Yes!" J.P. said under his breath, not realizing that everyone at the table had heard him.

"We all heard that, J.P." said Hannah.

"Heard what?" J.P. asked, as he noticed everyone at the table chuckling. "I didn't say anything."

"Sure," Hannah said. "I think Emily heard it, too."

"Heard what?" Emily replied, as everyone burst out laughing.

"Well, if you decide to run track in college, and if you decide to attend Concord, what would you like to study?" Mr. Galford continued.

"Probably physical therapy, athletic training, or something related to health care, like nursing," said Emily. "That has always been an interest of mine. My two best friends are going to major in health care, also.

Jenny is going to Marshall to study nursing, like her mother did. Her mom works for an ob-gyn doctor in Princeton. And Susan is already enrolled in the pre-med program at WVU. She wants to be a pediatrician and I know that she'll be a great one. She's our valedictorian and the smartest person in our graduating class."

"That all sounds good," said Bob. "It seems like so many young people today don't think much about what they will do with their lives. But I can tell that you've definitely been thinking about it."

"What about you, Hannah?" asked Emily. "Any thoughts about college or a career?"

"A little bit," replied Hannah. "I think I want to teach, like my mom does, but probably in high school and not grade school. But lately I've just been thinking about the prom and my dress; things like that."

"The prom?" asked J.P. "I can't believe my little sis is going to the prom."

"After all, J.P., I am a junior this year," said Hannah.

"I know, but you're still my little sis," J.P. said. "And I'm not there to protect you anymore."

"I don't need protecting," Hannah replied. "Anyway, Chip can protect me, if I need it."

"Chip?" asked J.P. "Don't tell me you're going to the prom with Chip Taylor?"

"That's right," said Hannah. "Why would you care who I go to prom with?"

"I guess I don't, in a way," J.P. said. "But Chip Taylor isn't who I would have picked for you to go with."

"Isn't that the boy who you got into a shoving match with a couple of years ago in the summer basketball league?" asked Bob.

"I don't remember, dad," answered J.P. "It's not important. So, Hannah, you want to be a teacher like mom is?" J.P. asked, as he changed the subject.

"That's what I'm thinking right now," said Hannah, "but I still have quite a while to figure that out. I like math, so I could probably teach algebra or trigonometry or something, and maybe help coach the girls track team. I think that all of the schools that I could possibly attend have teacher education programs. And if I can get Emily to help me with my distance training, who knows, maybe I could run track or cross country at Concord? That way I could keep an eye on you, brother."

Everyone had to laugh at that last comment. "Maybe you could bring Chip along to help protect you," J.P. said sarcastically.

Soon the group was finished eating and ready to depart the restaurant. "I can drop J.P. off at his motel," said Al Adams. "It won't be out of our way. That is, as long as everyone is okay with that."

"I think that is a good plan, dad," Emily readily agreed.

"Me, too," J.P. quickly chimed in, as he turned to smile at Emily.

"Well, it was certainly good to meet you and Hannah," said Al. "Hopefully, we can do this again and maybe Rita and Linda will be there then."

"That would be nice," Bob replied. "It was good talking with you and Emily, too."

Everyone left the restaurant to return to their cars. Bob and Al brought up the rear. "Let's stay in contact," Al said to Bob. "If things proceed with these two lovebirds, like it appears it might," motioning toward Emily and J.P. who were now holding hands as they walked, "then we will need to talk from time to time."

"Agreed," Bob said. "Safe travels home for you and Emily."

"Thanks," Al replied. "You, too."

"Good luck tomorrow," Bob told his son, as they all got to their cars. "I wish we could be there to watch the games, but we have to go over to Covington to get your mom and to check on your granddad."

"Thanks, dad," J.P. said, "and I'm glad you and Hannah could come today. I'll call you tomorrow evening after we get back to Athens and let you know how the games turned out. And tell mom and granddad I said hello."

"Will do," Bob replied.

"Goodbye, sis," J.P. said to Hannah. "I enjoyed watching you run yesterday and thanks for coming to my games today. And keep an eye on that Chip Taylor. I wouldn't trust him much, but maybe you know him better than I do."

"I'm sure I do," replied Hannah. "And I'll be sure to tell him you said hello, too," she said with a grin.

"I don't think I would do that," said J.P. "Better just let that ride."

Bob and Hannah drove away, as J.P. and Emily got close together in the backseat of her dad's car. Looking in the rearview mirror, Al asked with a smile, "Would one of you like to ride up front with me?"

"Not me," replied Emily.

"Me neither," answered J.P. "I'm comfortable back here," as he gave Emily a little hug.

"Fine, I guess I'll just be the chauffeur, then," Al said.

Shortly Al pulled into the parking lot where the Concord baseball team was staying. "I enjoyed watching you play today, J.P.," said Mr. Adams. "Maybe I can come over to Athens and watch another game later on."

"That would be great," J.P. replied. "And Emily could come, too. Right?"

"Definitely," Emily answered hurriedly.

"But I think we only have another weekend doubleheader at home before the conference tournament," explained J.P. "I'll check the schedule, but I think we play Glenville at home next weekend. The week after that, the tournament starts. We won't know who we play until after next weekend's games, but the tournament is supposed to be held in Beckley this year."

"We could go watch the tournament, too," said Emily. "Beckley is close to where we live."

"We'll see," replied her dad. "But we could probably swing that."

"Well, I'd better let coach know that I'm back," said J.P. "Thanks for coming to my games."

"Good luck tomorrow," said Al.

"I'll walk in with J.P," Emily said as she opened the car door. "I wouldn't want him to get lost," she giggled, looking over at J.P.

"Don't take too long," her dad said, "we need to get on the road home."

Emily and J.P. walked in to the motel lobby, said their goodbye's, and promised to call each other the next week. Before she turned to leave, Emily leaned up and gave J.P. a kiss on the cheek. He was not expecting that, but was happy that she did. Without even thinking, he leaned down and gave her a short kiss on the lips.

Emily turned to leave and thought, 'that was great,' while J.P. wondered if he had done the right thing.

Emily got back in her dad's car, the front seat this time, with a smile on her face.

"I saw that," said her dad.

"Saw what?" asked Emily.

"Never mind," Al said, "but I know what I saw."

"Well, whatever it was that you *think* you saw, you don't need to mention it to mom," Emily said. "Deal?"

"Deal," her dad answered.

On the drive home, they talked about Emily's upcoming graduation and whether or not she should run track in college. She would have to make a decision soon, as well as choosing between Pikeville and Concord. About halfway home, Emily dozed off; she had had a busy, tiring, and eventful last few days.

*　*　*　*　*　*　*

Concord again split the doubleheader with Charleston on Sunday, winning the first game 5-4 and dropping the second game 6-1. J.P. had two hits and a walk in four at bats the first game, while scoring two runs. He went 1-4 in the second game and Concord had trailed from the second inning on, never able to get a threatening rally started.

J.P. called Emily once he got back to his room on the Concord campus. They talked for half an hour and decided they would talk again on Tuesday. A short while later, J.P.'s parents called him and gave a good report on his grandfather.

After church on Sunday morning, Bob and Hannah drove over to Woody Johnson's home in Covington and found him in good spirits, although still a little sore and tender in his stomach area. Linda decided to stay one more night with her dad just to make sure he was going to be able to do the routine things necessary for someone who lived alone. Bob would drive back over on Monday evening after he got off work to pick her up and bring her home.

*   *   *   *   *   *   *

On Monday evening Bob arrived to pick up Linda. Woody was sorry to see his daughter leave, but he was feeling much better and he knew that she had things to do in Lewisburg. They said their goodbye's and the Galford's headed home.

"Your dad seems to be doing well," Bob said to Linda as they drove back west on Interstate 64. "I think he'll be fine, as long as he doesn't over-do things for a couple of weeks."

"I think you're right," she replied. "He's pretty stubborn though and who knows what he might try to do before he should. Sometimes he forgets how old he is," Linda laughed. "I did have a talk with him about moving to Lewisburg and for the first time ever, he said it might not be a bad idea. He said he'd think about it."

"Well, that's definitely a first," said Bob. "The couple of times I've mentioned it in the past he gave me a dirty look and said a quick no. One time he said something like I should mind my own business," Bob said, smiling.

"Really?" replied Linda. "You never told me that."

"Didn't think you needed to know," said Bob. "By the way I wanted to tell you that it seems as though J.P. has a new girlfriend."

"Well, it's about time," said Linda. "I guess it doesn't surprise me. It's been over a year since he and Barb broke up and he said he was done with girls."

"Yeah, I know," Bob said. "We always thought he and Barb were in it for the long haul. They seemed so happy together and had dated since junior high school."

"When she got that academic scholarship to Georgetown and he decided to play baseball at Concord, it was just too drastic a change for them to handle, I guess," replied Linda. "It was probably for the best anyway. Tell me, who's his new girlfriend, someone he met at Concord?"

"Not exactly," Bob answered. "It's a girl he met at Hannah's track meet in Charleston and they've only known each other for, let's see now, three days. But you should see the way they look at each other. J.P.'s got it bad, I think. And Emily does, too, from what I can tell. I just met her on Saturday."

"Emily, huh?" And three days!" said Linda. "This is a surprise. Tell me more. Where does she go to college?"

"Actually, she's just getting ready to graduate from high school," Bob explained. "She ran the 1600 and 3200 meter races for PikeView in the AA portion of the state meet. Hannah told me that Emily finished second in the 1600 and third in the 3200. Evidently, she has a couple of offers to run track in college."

"PikeView; I'm not sure where that's located. Isn't that up around Wheeling?" asked Linda.

"No, it's actually close to Concord, down near Princeton," said Bob.

"Don't tell me," said Linda. "Concord is one of the colleges that have offered her a track scholarship."

"You got it," Bob replied. "I don't think it's definite yet, but the way they were hanging on to each other after the baseball game Saturday, my guess is that is where she will go to college."

"This all seems kind of sudden," Linda said. "Is that all you know? Like, how exactly did they meet?"

"Not really clear on that part," said Bob. "That's pretty much all I know at this point," replied Bob. "He'll have to fill us in, I guess. Hannah may know more."

"So, how did you meet her?" asked Linda.

"She and her dad drove up from Princeton on Saturday morning to watch J.P.'s baseball game," Bob answered. "Evidently Al, that's Emily's dad, is a big baseball fan and he had even gone over to watch Concord play a couple of games earlier in the season. He said they only live 10 miles or so from Athens. He seems like a nice guy.

"Whenever Hannah and I got to the game in Charleston on Saturday," Bob continued, "Emily was down near the visitor's dugout talking with J.P. That's when I met her, and then her dad. We talked some and then we all had dinner together after the ballgames. And by the way, Al is a forester; he knows Rod Lathems."

"That's interesting," said Linda. "Small world, I guess. Well, this is all a surprise, but I guess we'll learn more as time goes on."

*   *   *   *   *   *   *

That following weekend, Concord finished its regular season baseball schedule by winning three out of four games at home against Glenville. The Mountain Lions finished the season in the middle of the conference standings and were scheduled to face Wheeling in the first round of the tournament in Beckley on that next Thursday.

Bob, Linda, and Hannah were able to go to Athens for the doubleheader against Glenville on Sunday. They had not gone down on Saturday because they decided to drive over to Covington and check on Woody and see how he was doing. He seemed to be doing great and they were all relieved that he had come through his operation with no complications.

Emily and her dad attended all four games against Glenville that weekend and Rita had gone over with them for the Sunday afternoon games. The Galford and the Adams families had a chance to talk, get to know each other better, and have dinner on Sunday evening before they all headed home. They all seemed to get along very well. And it didn't escape anyone's notice that J.P. and Emily barely knew what anyone else was talking about – their conversation and their eyes were focused on one another.

*   *   *   *   *   *   *

The Concord baseball team was on a hot streak in the Mountain East Conference double-elimination tournament. They won three straight games against Wheeling, Charleston, and Alderson-Broaddus, and advanced to the finals undefeated on the winners bracket side. There they faced the powerful West Virginia State team, which had actually dropped its tournament opener before fighting back to reach the finals.

Unfortunately, by the time the finals rolled around, Concord's pitching, which was not as deep as West Virginia State's, was pretty much depleted and the Yellow Jackets won the final two games convincingly. West Virginia State advanced to the NCAA Division II Regional Tournament, but there they were beaten by a team from the always strong Pennsylvania State Athletic Conference.

After his successful freshman season, J.P. was named to the MEC All-Conference second team, as well as Freshman of the Year in a vote by the conference coaches.

J.P.'s coach finalized the plans for him to play for the Bluefield team in the collegiate summer league. He obtained approval from the athletic department for J.P. to stay in his garage apartment for the summer. He also was able to put J.P. on a full scholarship beginning with his sophomore season.

And as hoped, the Bluefield team traveled to face Princeton in the summer league twice, once in June and once in July. J.P. was leading the league in walks and stolen bases and batting around .280. The pitching in this league was a little better than he had ever faced, plus it was taking some effort getting used to the wooden bats again. In the college season all the teams used aluminum bats. Emily and her parents attended all four of the games that Bluefield played in Princeton. She and her dad also went down to Bluefield twice to see J.P. play a game against a team from Tennessee and a team from Virginia.

J.P. was pretty busy with his games and practices, but he drove over to see Emily as often as he could. And she came to Athens when their schedules allowed. They were growing closer and closer and each one thought that this was the best person they had ever dated. Their future together looked bright.

J.P. had been able to attend Emily's graduation at PikeView High School and the very next day Emily signed a scholarship offer to run track for Concord. They were both so excited about that and Hannah was, too.

Emily invited Hannah to stay with the Adams' for a week twice during the summer. They worked out and trained together at both the PikeView and the Concord facilities. Hannah learned a lot from Emily and with the targeted workouts and conditioning drills, she was getting stronger and stronger. Her times had already improved considerably in both the 1600 and 3200 meter distances. She now had high hopes for her senior season in high school, as well as for hopefully running track in college.

In August, before school started and after J.P.'s summer baseball league had ended, he and Emily traveled to Lewisburg for a Friday through Monday visit with the Galford's. They all had a chance to get to know each other even better and also traveled to Covington to spend an afternoon with J.P.'s grandfather, who seemed to be fully recovered from his earlier operation.

Woody and Emily seemed to really hit it off and right before the Galford's headed home, he pulled J.P. to the side and said, "I think you've got yourself a winner there son. I like her. She reminds me a lot of your grandmother when we were young. You'd better hold on to that one."

"I plan to, granddad," said J.P. "And thanks for the kind words about Emily."

Not long after that visit, J.P. and Emily announced to everyone that they were formally a couple, not that anyone had thought they weren't. But this seemed to take it one step further in their relationship.

*   *   *   *   *   *   *

Classes began at Concord for the pair and Hannah had started her senior year at Greenbrier East High School. The Galford and Adams families had settled into their normal routines again.

Emily soon began training for the Mountain Lions' indoor track season, which ran from December through February with five or six meets. It then almost immediately transitioned into the outdoor season, which would run from March – May. It was quite exhausting for her and quite a step up in intensity from high school. Still, she enjoyed it and found plenty of study time to do well in her classes.

J.P.'s baseball team also had fall practices, several intrasquad scrimmages, and an intense indoor conditioning regimen once winter set in. He was looking forward to having a great sophomore season.

The couple spent any spare time they had together; and sometimes in the library studying for their classes. They grew closer and fell more and more in love as the months went on. This seemed to be headed for a long term relationship and hopefully marriage if things worked out.

And it had all begun after meeting in the food line at Laidley Field during the state track meet.

POSTSCRIPT

I hope you enjoyed reading these four West Virginia romance stories for young readers as much as I enjoyed writing them.

In the future you will read about other young romances from various areas of the state, including the northern panhandle; the southern coalfields; the central counties; the mountains; from the Ohio River to the Virginia and Maryland borders; from the counties that border Kentucky, Pennsylvania, and Ohio; and all points in between – tales of young love in the Mountain State occur everywhere.

You can visit the website below for summaries of my previous 12 books, as well as other author information. You can also leave me a message.

I look forward to hearing from you.

The website address is:

https://dankincaid,com

OTHER BOOKS BY DAN KINCAID

The Penicillin Kids, the 1966 West Virginia Class AA State Basketball Champions, 2015.

Your.....Wayne National Forest, Volumes I, II, & III, three books of the author's weekly Ohio newspaper columns written from 1981 - 1990, published in 2016, 2017, & 2018 respectively.

Your.....Chattahoochee National Forest, a historical collection of the author's weekly Georgia newspaper columns from December 1978 – June 1980, published in 2016.

Kade Holley, Forest Ranger, Vol. I, fictional accounts of Kade's adventures on National Forests in Minnesota, Ohio, North Carolina, and Washington, 2017.

Kade Holley, Forest Ranger, Vol. II, fictional accounts of Kade's adventures on National Forests in Georgia, West Virginia, Minnesota, Ohio, and Colorado, 2018.

A Gift to the Nation-From Ohio and Wayne National Forest, the 1987 Capitol Christmas Tree, 2019.

Kade Holley, Forest Ranger, Vol. III, fictional accounts of Kade's adventures on National Forests in West Virginia, Georgia, Ohio, and Minnesota, 2019.

West Virginia Romances: Tales of Young Love in the Mountain State, Volume I, 2020.

Softball in The Villages® Community: Senior Softball Heaven, 2020.

The Great Outdoors newspaper columns written (from 1985 – 1990) by the author, 2021.

All books are available at Amazon.com, Booksamillion.com, and Barnesandnoble.com

AUTHOR BIO – Dan Kincaid

The author, a West Virginia native, embarks on writing volume two of his teenage romance series in: **West Virginia Romances – Tales of Young Love in the Mountain State**.

His previous 12 books primarily revolved around his experiences during a 31-year career with the U.S. Forest Service at National Forest locations in West Virginia, Ohio, Minnesota, Georgia, and North Carolina, as well as various other temporary assignments in Colorado, Kentucky, California, Indiana, Washington, Michigan, Montana, and Tennessee. In addition he spent several years with state forestry agencies in West Virginia and Ohio, as well as in private sector forestry.

Kincaid received a Bachelor's of Science degree in Forest Resource Management from West Virginia University; a Master's degree in Forestry/ Environmental Management from Duke University; and a Teaching Certification for Biology and General Science from Marietta College in Ohio.

Kincaid and his wife, Vicki, are currently retired and living in Florida, where he contemplates writing his next volumes of teenage romance stories and forest ranger adventures.

Made in the USA
Columbia, SC
04 April 2022

58315647R00098